Between Heartbeats

NETTLEBY TRILOGY - BOOK THREE

ROSIE CHAPEL

ULFIRE PTY LTD

First printing 2024
ISBN (E-book): 978-1-7635407-7-4
ISBN (Print): 978-1-7635407-8-1

Ulfire Pty. Ltd.
P.O. Box 1481
South Perth
WA 6951
Australia

www.rosiechapel.com

Cover Design: R Norman
Cover Images Courtesy: Canva/Deposit Photos/Pixabay
(Artists: Evasilchenko, Mickey Mikolauskas, and Tesfay Haile)
Internal images: Canva/Deposit Photos.
Designed in Canva
Created using appropriate licences.

Acknowledgments

My thanks to…

My husband for his unfailing support.

Dad for telling me about Joseph Elliott, my great grandfather whose story gave rise to this trilogy. I wish you were here to read the final instalment.

Mum and Melanie for putting up with my nonsense

Graham from Fading Street Publishing Services for wielding his editing wand.

For
Dad, in absentia,
and Uncle Robin...
...whose grandfather inspired this trilogy

Author's Note

During World War One, medical care was, in the main, the responsibility of the Royal Army Medical Corps (RAMC). Entrusted with maintaining the health and fighting strength of the forces in the field, they also ensured the sick or injured were treated and evacuated or returned to their division as quickly as possible.

Every battalion had a medical officer, assisted by more than a dozen stretcher-bearers, whose first task was to instal a Regimental Aid Post near the front line... the first link in a complex chain of evacuation.

NB: Not all the injured went through every stage.

The Evacuation Chain
Regimental Aid Post
Advanced Dressing Station
Field Ambulance
Casualty Clearing Station
Ambulance Trains and Barges
Base Hospital
Convalescent Depots

Home hospital
Command Depot

Below is a more detailed description of the stations used in *Between Heartbeats*.

Regimental Aid Post (RAP)

A rudimentary care point proximate to the front line. RAP's were set up in compact spaces such as communication trenches, ruined buildings, dug outs or a deep shell hole. They had no holding capacity, but wounds were cleaned and dressed, pain relief administered, and basic first aid given.

Advanced Dressing Station (ADS)

Established by and run as part of the Field Ambulances (FA's). Typically about four to five hundred yards behind the RAP's, an Advanced Dressing Station was located anywhere which offered some protection from shellfire and air attack. Like the RAP's, the ADS was only a temporary staging post and, although better equipped than the former, could provide only limited medical care.

Field Ambulances (FA)

These were mobile front-line medical units (*not* a vehicle) for treating the wounded before they were transferred to a Casualty Clearing Station (CCS). As a general rule, each British division had three such units, plus a specialist medical sanitary unit and, at full strength, a Field Ambulance was staffed by 10 officers and 224 men.

An FA included stretcher-bearers, an operating tent, tented wards, nursing orderlies, cookhouse, washrooms and a horse drawn and/or motor ambulance. Each had a fully equipped surgical team and, by the autumn of 1915, trained nurses were assigned to some.

The men were assessed, using an innovative three-tier classification system called *triage* to prioritise cases, then labelled with information about their injuries and initial treatment. Any beyond help were medicated with morphia and other pain-killing drugs to ease their suffering.

Casualty Clearing Stations (CCS)

A Casualty Clearing Station was a small hospital, which received wounded from the field ambulances, ten to twenty miles behind the main dressing station, and preferably near railway junctions or rivers for ease of transfer.

Some were fortunate to be based in permanent buildings such as schools, convents, factories or sheds, but many were set up wherever space allowed, and consisted of large areas of tents, marquees and wooden huts, often covering half a square mile.

Each CCS sported operating theatres and wards, as well as a dispensary, medical stores, kitchens, sanitation, incineration plant, mortuary, ablution and sleeping quarters.

Between Heartbeats

The Nettleby Trilogy - Book Three

A WWI Novella

Prologue

31ˢᵗ December 1966
Polly

Fifty years — my head struggled to believe that was remotely possible, while my heart swelled at the fact it was true. Fifty years — to be honest, given where we said our vows, it is a miracle we lasted fifty days.

The face looking back at me through the mirror perched on my dressing table was youthful, unlined by the passage of time. In place of my white curls, ash-blonde hair scraped back into a tight bun and hidden under a white muslin cap. Soft skin, usually smeared with engine oil, instead of papery wrinkles.

When did I get old?

A hand landed on my shoulder, and my husband joined me on the cushioned seat, gathering me against him.

"Fifty years. Where did the time go?" He echoed my thoughts.

I studied his reflection… almost objectively. He still had that military bearing I so admired. His tanned features were no less creased than mine, but on men, it looked distinguished not aged. I ought to be annoyed by that, but I'm not. His hair, once so dark brown had greyed to a shade of rain splashed pewter and his rich brown eyes, now requiring spectacles, still twinkled.

In my mind's eye, I pictured us on our wedding day. Him in his uniform, me in my nurse's garb. Both of us ever-so slightly crumpled, our ecstatic smiles not quite able to erase the exhaustion etched on our faces.

I leant into him. "I'm not so sure I'm a fan of this whole growing old lark," I murmured.

He kissed my temple. "At least we are fortunate to be growing old, love. So many did not."

I swivelled to face him.

Our eyes met and the decades unravelled between us, catapulting us back to the cacophony that was France 1916.

One

1916 — Polly

Perfection is a September day on the Wold.

Above me, a clear blue sky, a gentler, paler hue than the dazzling azure we are blessed with during the height of summer, but no less beautiful.

Hazy sunshine bathed the scene in a mellow glow. The soft Lincolnshire air, which carried a hint of loamy earth, teemed with birds chasing insects as they prepared for their long flight south.

I lay back on my elbows and breathed deeply, filling my lungs with the scent of home.

Below me, nestled snugly in the landscape, Nettleby under Wold. A tiny village dating back to the dawn of time — if you believe the locals. True or not, there was something solid, dependable, and immutable about Nettleby, as though nothing could shake its foundations.

Ant-like figures moved across the neatly delineated fields.

If I strained my ears, I discerned the lowing of cows, and the occasional neigh of a horse.

The train hooted in the distance, and my gaze travelled to the puff of smoke pluming over the trees.

I lay back on the grass, shielding my eyes against the sun which had begun its slow descent to the far horizon where the sky was tinged with pink.

I loved my home.

"Just a little longer," I argued with the sensible part of me insisting I should not tarry, but I was unwilling to miss a single moment of this day. Tomorrow, I returned to training school, my dream of becoming a nurse inching ever closer.

The church clock behind me struck the hour, but I was shocked when it did not stop at five.

Bolting upright, I spun around, staring at the grey tower. The clanging got louder, the sky darkened, and the temperature plummeted.

Shivering, I jammed my fingers in my ears in a childish gesture to block out the din.

"Polly, wake, up. Polly." A hand landed on my shoulder, shaking me. The scene fractured and dissolved, vanishing into the void.

"No, no. Not yet, please..." I beseeched plaintively.

"Polly..."

I peeled back my eyelids to see Cilla Beckenham, my friend and tent-mate leaning over me.

"You were sleeping like the dead, my lass. Come on, up with you. You don't want the Dragon on your case."

Her gallows humour — given our location — tugged a

wry grin from my parched lips. "Any tea?" I asked hopefully, clinging to the last vestiges of my dream.

"Here." She handed me her battered, half-full beaker. "Sup that." Then yanked off my blanket.

"Oof, not fair," I groused and swallowed the swill the field kitchen referred to as tea in one gulp.

Washed, dressed, and my bed made to the Dragon's uncompromising guidelines, I trooped over to the canteen with Cilla where, after prayers, we demolished our breakfast in two shakes of a lamb's tail. No lingering over a meal.

The thud of the guns accompanied our dash across the compound to the wards.

I was a world away from a September day in Nettleby.

Here, it was June…

…and this was a Field Ambulance…

…in France.

The day began.

Despite the fact I had completed my training, I lacked any, for want of a better description, unsupervised experience. This seemed to fall, frustratingly, into a grey area in the eyes of the military nursing service who had to weigh up their needs against those of the civil hospitals who could not lose all their nurses.

For a while, I was at a loss as to how to proceed. Yes, it was much safer to stay in England, but I desperately wanted to help; for the sake of our little corner of the world if nothing else.

Then someone suggested I join the Volunteer Aid Detachment — or VADs as we were known. We were, I supposed, considered the jacks of all trades: nurses, cooks, cleaners, laundresses, maids, and… most importantly for me at least… drivers!

Initially posted to a Stationary Hospital, shortly thereafter, the group with whom I arrived was sent to a Casualty Clearing Station where, perforce, my nursing skills improved in leaps and bounds.

Six months ago, we were assigned to this Field Ambulance. Talk about eye-opening. Never in my life did I expect to see and hear what I have seen and heard. My mother would have a fit of the vapours if she had even half an inkling.

Confronting — definitely, harrowing — undoubtedly, but also extraordinarily rewarding.

I spent the majority of my days tending to the sick and injured… and, typically, our unit dealt with more of the latter than the former.

Don't get me wrong, I still shouldered my fair share of the assorted tasks expected of a VAD, but the number of qualified nurses was woefully inadequate.

Each of the four of us who shared a tent had done a minimum of a year's training, which the powers that be considered a boon — and you learnt very quickly at the front.

My aim, however, and the principal reason I volunteered, was to drive an ambulance. I contrived to spend most of my, negligible, spare time at the ambulance pool, badgering the mechanics and other drivers to teach me everything there was to know about our vehicles.

This sounded far grander than it was. In truth, someone had commandeered a corner of the encampment at the rear of the hospital and close to the road which allowed for rapid egress.

We were the privileged possessors of seven horse-drawn wagons, and four... yes, *four* motorised ambulances. I loved the horses, such brave and noble creatures, but these vehicles were lifesavers... when they worked.

Time was of the essence here.

The faster wounded soldiers were conveyed to a Field Ambulance... a medical unit not a vehicle... the better their chance of survival. The horse-drawn wagons took twice as long to cover the distance, as the motorised ambulances — a delay which could mean the difference between life and death.

I was fortunate — a dubious appellation — to be posted here, after the sequence for withdrawing the injured had already been established. It must have been a nightmare at the outbreak of the war when everything was trial and error.

Now, it ran like a well-oiled wheel... almost, which did not equate to being safe. Except the base hospitals, every medical station proximate to the front line was vulnerable.

The chain of evacuation began at the Regimental Aid Post. These were found, more often than not, in a dug out or along one of the communications trenches or occasionally, if they were lucky, a ruined building.

Conditions were appalling and there was no holding capacity. Diligently, but swiftly, the wounded were triaged — the latest byword applied to the assessment of casualties according to urgency. Rudimentary first aid was administered where appropriate, stretcher cases were transferred to the Advanced Dressing Station, and the rest returned to their units.

Dressing Stations, an extension of Field Ambulances, were only marginally better equipped than the aid posts but, set up a reasonable distance from the trenches, gained some respite from shell fire. Once assessed, any patients deemed to require further treatment were transported to us at the Field Ambulance.

We acted as a middleman, so to speak. Although lacking the resources available to a Casualty Clearing Station, the next stop up the line, we sported an operating tent, wards, and everything necessary to sustain a small hospital. Major surgery was possible if we did not think we could get the injured person to the CCS, and we were righteously proud of our survival rate.

We had moved three times since I was posted to this FA, but word from the top was that we would be here for the foreseeable future.

"Polly, you got a minute?" a voice hailed me from the door of the operating tent.

"Captain?" I hurried over, automatically brushing my hands over my uniform, and making sure my cap was in place.

The rest of the morning vanished in a flurry of activity. Sometimes, I wanted to slow down the madness but, to be honest, busy days were better than slow ones. They gave me no time to think.

Two

June 1916 — Polly

Dearest Lizzie,

My sincere apologies for the tardiness of my response to your lovely letter. News from home never fails to lift my spirits. Your description of the flowers carpeting the hedgerows was so vivid, I could picture them, even smell their fragrance. Much more palatable than the scene in front of me. More on that later.

We have moved again. I suspect something major is afoot, although nobody is bothering to tell us. No change there. Our last station was short-lived and utter luxury compared with where we are now, but it is what it is. At least we are safe here.

afe, a relative concept. I paused and tapped my pencil abstractedly on the notepaper.

Our previous quarters, an old chateau, had been an unexpected sojourn and some distance from the front line.

The daily routine was no less arduous or challenging, but the surrounds made it just that bit easier to bear. An image formed in my head.

The elegant facade of the grand old building, glowing pale gold in the afternoon sun, floating in acres of lush gardens... most not commandeered by the various military divisions.

A momentary idyll — if you ignored the rows of laundry, sheets, and bandages flapping in the gentle breeze, a sharp reminder of our presence.

"Nurse, nurse..." a hoarse voice penetrated my daydreams. Dropping my letter on the wooden chair, I hurried over to where Private Eric Burston lay. Poor bugger lost a leg a week ago to a stray German mortar and was still fighting infection. It was touch and go for a while, but he refused to succumb, and the doctors believed he had turned the corner and was on the slow road to recovery.

All being well, he would be transferred to a Casualty Clearing Station within a couple of days. The only reason he was still here was because, currently, hostilities had dwindled to a few skirmishes, and we had spare beds.

Not that this was expected to last.

"What is it, Private?" I asked. "Thirsty? In pain?"

"Thirsty."

His jug was empty. I had topped it up only an hour ago. Not necessarily cause for concern, but I added it to my mental checklist… just in case… hopefully nothing sinister lurked.

I replenished the jug from the huge drum at the end of the ward, doing the same with three others I grabbed on my way to save another journey.

"Here." I helped him to sit upright and handed him the tumbler. "Try not to gulp it, you'll get hiccups," I cautioned with a grin.

His pale lips curved slightly. It was the first time I'd seen the faintest trace of a smile. Another win.

He returned the cup, which I refilled and placed within easy reach on the little table next to his cot.

"Thank you, nurse," he rasped. "Sorry to disturb you." He nodded towards my chair where the flimsy sheets of paper were lifting in the slight breeze wafting through the flaps of the tent.

"You did not disturb me. Just a letter home."

"Where is home?"

"Tiny village in Lincolnshire. I doubt you will have heard of it."

"Try me."

"Nettleby under Wold." Just saying the words made me feel warm inside and triggered a flood of memories.

"Near Wrawby?" Private Burston quirked an inquisitive brow.

I stared at him in surprise. "You *have* heard of it. Well, I never."

"I'm from Grimsby," his features lifted, "and have family in Wrawby."

"Ahh, so you'll be with one of the Lincolnshire regiments." I made it a statement not a question.

"Tenth Battalion." There was more than a hint of pride in his reply.

Why did that sound familiar? I rolled the name of the regiment around my head, and it came to me.

"The Grimsby Chums?" I hazarded, referring to one of the Pals battalions, and the only one permitted the moniker of Chums. So named because they comprised men who had all enlisted together, with the assurance they would serve alongside their friends and neighbours, instead of being allocated arbitrarily.

"The very same."

"I should have recognised your accent. Cannot think why I did not."

"It's this attractive husky voice I seem blessed with at the moment." He started to laugh then grimaced.

I patted his hand. "Eminently possible, and try not to talk too much, you need to rest. Are you in pain?"

"Nothing, I can't handle," he said stoically. "Tell me about Nettleby." His words starting to slur as exhaustion prowled.

"Only if you promise to close your eyes and try to sleep."

"Promise." Obediently, he did as I had bidden. I tucked the blanket around him and began to describe my favourite place in the whole world.

I talked until certain slumber had claimed him. With light fingers, I checked his pulse; steady and quite strong. Placing the back of my hand on his forehead, I was pleased to note the heat indicating a fever lurked had cooled to almost normal and, if I wasn't mistaken, his features were less pallid.

Standing, I walked along the cots, running my eyes over each occupant. We were quiet at the moment… thank goodness. Not that anyone was fool enough to remark on it, that was asking for trouble.

I chatted with those who were awake. Most would rejoin their regiments before the week was out.

While they were raring to return to their mates, I wanted

to send the lot of them home forthwith. Barely more than children, youthful faces already aging, eyes haunted.

The rumours regarding an imminent and huge offensive drifted through my head for the umpteenth time, and my stomach knotted. *How long could we keep fighting? Was there any chance we were going to win this damn war.* I had to believe we would, that the allies could stem the tide, that good would trump evil, even while acknowledging the enemy probably believed they were on the side of good and we were the evil monsters who dared stand in their way.

I dragged my mind away from what I could not change and, ensuring my presence was not required, resumed my seat to continue with my letter.

For want of something to write, I described the chateau; it made for more interesting reading than trench warfare.

I skirted around the reality of my day-to-day life at the Field Ambulance, preferring to focus on the often-humorous exploits of those among whom I worked.

It was a way to relieve the intolerable tension, and I could not imagine anyone wanting to read harrowing tales of blood, guts, and gore.

Lizzie, I've included herewith a letter for Maisie. Please would you be so kind as to pass it on? Envelopes are like hen's teeth, and we've been told their availability is likely to get worse rather than better.

My shift is almost over. I'm looking forward to a hot meal, a cup of tea, and a long bath. Might get the first two, the last is wishful thinking. Oh well, two out of three isn't to be sniffed at.

I hope this finds you and Joe well.

À bientôt,
Polly.

I folded it neatly, squeezed it into the drab green envelope alongside Maisie's letter, and slipped it into my pocket ready to add to the stack of mail waiting to be collected.

Three

1ˢᵗ July 1916 — Gommecourt
Thad

We had done everything humanly… and occasionally inhumanly… possible to prepare for the offensive.

Why did it sit ill on my shoulders?

Because we were doomed. After what I had witnessed, I would have to be an imbecile to accept the oft repeated assurances about how we would prevail. Not that I was about to voice my concerns. Stiff upper lip and all that.

Exhaustion gnawed at my bones, but sleep was an elusive bedmate this night. Tactics from the reasonable to the ridiculous had been bouncing around my head since sundown, the ramifications becoming more catastrophic as the hours ticked by.

I do not know why I kept second guessing myself. I had our orders; they were succinct, stark, and simple enough that an inebriated donkey would understand them. The top brass left no room for mistakes.

Of course, I knew why — these were *my* men, and it was my job to get them home in as close to one piece as I could manage. *One piece…* I slapped my forehead.

In a vain attempt to distract myself, I had spent the night checking the trenches to make sure our routes through the labyrinthine network were as unobstructed as possible. Speed would be crucial today.

In the distance, a faint sliver of pink light heralded the sunrise. Shivering, and not just from the slightly damp air of the pre-dawn, I returned to my dugout and supped what was left of my tea. Cold and stewed it might be, but it was still tea, and not to be wasted.

Leaning on the crumbling wooden frame of the bunker, I studied the sky. It was going to be a glorious day.

How ironic.

I shook my head, keenly aware the magnificence of this July morning would be the *last* thing on the minds of my men — yet, however untenable the notion, for so many it would be their last day. Quixotically, I hoped some of its beauty might help ameliorate the inevitable suffering, ushering them to whichever heaven they believed in painlessly… simultaneously berating myself for being an idiot.

In the quiet before the storm, I prayed.

The sound of shuffling feet jerked me back to the moment.

Turning, I put my battered tin mug on the table — in actuality, three small sections of duckboard, hastily cobbled together, but exceedingly useful — inside the dugout, and murmured a greeting to one or two pale-faced soldiers as they stretched weary limbs.

. . .

At six, I assembled my sergeants to reiterate the plan for the hundredth time.

"Are you clear?" I asked. "Unless otherwise ordered, we are delegated to the reserve to deliver supplies. Tell the lads to keep their heads down. It's too easy to forget when you're rushing to deliver equipment. You would be wise to do the same. Our friends over there will want to disrupt the supply chains as much as they want to halt those going over the top."

I could not prevent the weighty sigh which all but blew over the men closest to me. "I'm not going to lie. This is huge, and surviving the day will take a miracle, but we are the Lincolnshires, and we do not dodge our duty... although dodging bullets is highly recommended."

A soft hum of laughter rippled through the men circling me. I swung my gaze across them, imprinting their tired faces into my mind which was already calculating how many letters I'd be writing by the end of the week.

"Right, away with you and remember what I said. Stay low, stay safe."

At seven, we were in position, assigned to the 138th Brigade as a carrying party. Outwardly, less dangerous than going over the top, in reality, we were equally vulnerable. The aim of both sides was sabotage and slaughter, and if that meant disrupting the supply lines — so be it. Brutal but accurate.

The worst thing about this war... if, at this point, one was able to differentiate between the diminishing levels of turpitude ... was the collapse of humanity. It was plain, we had learnt nothing from earlier conflicts.

In fact, from an objective perspective, one could be forgiven for thinking that every other battle from the dawn of time was merely practice. Each one, a minor precursor to this — the last great war of our world.

Thad Jenkins, what on earth has got into you this morning? I chastised internally. *You sound like a Penny Dreadful swallowed a Boy's Own.*

Unable to dismiss my fanciful notions completely, I did succeed in banishing them to the furthest recesses of my mind where they muttered balefully but did not interfere with my concentration.

Quietly, I walked the trench, giving what I hoped were words of encouragement.

Twenty minutes later, as smoke drifted up from the left flank, a silent wave of soldiers swarmed over the top to take up position in no man's land.

My heart thudded so loudly, I expected to receive an order to muffle it — surprised when none came. I looked at my watch: 7:28. One final check. I nodded at my men and sent up another prayer for their protection.

7:30. All hell broke loose.

When I reviewed the day, as I prepared my report, the best phrase I could come up with was organised chaos. We worked tirelessly to ensure everything required was provided almost before it was needed.

A non-stop train of perfectly synchronised soldiers weaving back and forth, conveying weapons and ammunition to their comrades at the front, to the backdrop of explosions and flying shrapnel, interspersed with the staccato rattle of gunfire and unceasing screams of the dying.

"Come on, Lord," I sent up the petition, even as I saw a man fall to a bullet — although, from my vantage point whether friend or foe was impossible to discern. "The fault of this does not lie with them."

An entreaty immediately forgotten because I was handed a new order by a harried radio operator.

"What?" I caught the lad by his shoulder, certain I had misheard.

The main assault by the companies we were supporting, despite early gains, had failed, and we went from keeping the supplies moving, to holding what had been named the Midland Trench.

I say 'we' — I did not have to go, but what sort of example was I setting if I loitered in comparative safety at the rear of the network, while they faced the enemy?

The damn Hun pinned us down for the rest of the day. Sadly, we lost ten men and another wounded, who we ferried to the stretcher bearers before he was coated in filth. He was in good hands now; the Field Ambulances were miracle workers.

Dusk was a welcome sight… or so we hoped.

The same radio operator loomed up like a shadow. "Sorry, sir, but…"

I could see he was reluctant to continue.

"What is it, Nicholls?" I pressed.

"Yer've bin ordered ter relieve the 139th and be ready to go forward with the Leicesters to reach those allied troops believed to be holding out in the German's front-line trenches."

I stared at him as though he was speaking a foreign language.

"I beg your pardon?" I strove to remain calm.

Slowly and clearly, he repeated the order.

I pinched the bridge of my nose. "But the 139th are at Foncquevillers," I said, stupidly.

"Sir," was his less than satisfactory reply.

"Thank you, Nicholls." I gave him the response he was waiting for, as though it was in any doubt. What did they think I would say? "Err, sorry, we've had enough and have decided to go home."

I rejoined the men who looked at me expectantly. Masking my true feelings, I gave the order.

Absolute silence.

"I know," was the best I could manage.

Four

Evening — 1ˢᵗ July 1916
Foncquevillers
Thad

As the gloaming darkened to night, a trivial conversation developed into a serious discussion — the substance controversial, bordering on treasonous.

I listened, more to pass the time than for any other reason… and ensure they kept their voices down. I had no mind for any of them to end up in front of a firing squad.

Neither were they wrong. If each man laid down his arms and walked away, there would be no war; the bloodshed would stop in an instant and, surely the powers that be would not stoop to declaring every soldier a traitor.

Then again… I did not finish that thought.

I scoured my brain for a less barbarous topic, caught off guard when Sylvia's face chased through my mind. Curious, I had not thought of my wife for some considerable time. *Did that mean my death was imminent? Was she waiting to escort me across the divide?*

"Still with the introspection, Thad," I tutted.

I shifted my weight, trying to get comfortable, as memories of my only other visit to France reared up. It was our honeymoon. I had scrimped and saved every spare penny for months before we got married, determined to take my new wife to Paris. The city of romance and love.

It did not disappoint.

Around every corner was some new delight. Churches, parks, leafy streets. The Eiffel Tower, the Notre Dame, the Arc de Triomphe — we saw them all at least once. I was fascinated by the elegance of the architecture along the Seine... and the Seine... oh, the Seine. I could watch the gracious glide of its waters all day.

We treated ourselves to café and croissants every morning, drank wine every evening, ate so much exotic food, I thought I might burst. Made love until dawn... and repeat, and repeat, and repeat...

A spasm of melancholy washed over me, as I registered, it was more than five years since Sylvia had died. *Five years!* Where did they go? It seemed forever yet barely the blink of an eye.

Was there any chance... assuming I escaped this nightmare... of finding another love?

Snap out of it, I remonstrated inwardly. *Come on man, you are supposed to be a Warrant Officer in charge of a regiment, not a love-lorn widower. You were lucky to find one love, wishing for a second is plain greedy.*

The next few hours were a monumental farce... the politest description I could summon up.

Contrary to our intel, the enemy's defences at the other

side of no man's land, remained intact. The trenches, we had been assured were in the control of the allies… were not.

Had the volley of expletives I bit back been bullets, we would have won the bloody war right then.

My men were stuck, with no alternative but to lie down and wait until something changed or a retreat was called.

Lie down and wait!

You could not make this up.

Never have I felt so powerless. Watching the Germans strafe the ground with a hail of gunfire at even the slightest movement was gut-wrenching, and I knew the injury toll was mounting.

Throughout that night, which, to this day, I vow was the longest of my life, I exhorted — under my breath, of course; I was not addled enough to raise my voice and reveal our position — for everyone in no man's land to play possum. An amusing phrase and a favourite of an uncle who had visited America years ago because, apparently, opossums feign death when threatened. If it worked for the beleaguered opossums...

The agonised cries and moans dwindled as the first rays of sunlight broke the horizon to steal across the narrow strip of land where so many lay trapped.

The retreat was called… finally.

A Red Cross flag was hoisted, providing a semblance of protection, and a swarm of soldiers squirming like giant centipedes returned to the relative safety of the trenches.

Several were able to drag their wounded comrades with them, but not all. More than I cared to count remained where they fell, some of whom were taken prisoner.

. . .

To my abject relief, a forty-eight-hour, uni-lateral ceasefire meant rescue parties could recover both survivors and bodies. That the conflict could be suspended for this task, merely highlighted the utter fatuity of war.

The brush of bodies across the dew-laden grass stirred up sweet fragrances from the myriad wildflowers scattered about. While not enough to mask the metallic stench of blood and death, the scent brought to mind my thoughts of the previous dawn.

My stomach roiled and I clenched my jaw to quell rising nausea. *So much for being impervious.* Forcing aside my own anger and sorrow, I focussed on helping the stretcher bearers convey casualties to the raft of medics waiting at the aid post.

We worked like trojans, desperate to retrieve every last soldier we could find, even if that meant naught but a shoe or a badge.

The day was waning. The underside of the clouds were streaked with purple, orange, and pink as the sun disappeared. In the encroaching twilight, the peace was ruptured by the chatter of gunfire.

Dear Lord, are they so eager to resume the killing?

Fred Cuthbert and Charlie Townsend were carrying an unconscious soldier to the ladder. Jack Philips, and a handful of others on their heels.

"These are the last," Jack puffed, the young private looking as haggard as I felt.

"Careful now, gently," the stretcher bearer cautioned as the patient was lowered to willing arms.

Charlie slid down the ladder.

Fred was about to follow when, without warning, he roared like a wounded bull and pitched headfirst into the trench.

"Orderly," I yelled, then dropped to my knees alongside the man who in that moment reverted to being my friend, not my subordinate. "Fred." I checked his pulse; it was erratic but strong, which was of some relief. "Come on, Fred, Maisie will have my guts if you die on me."

I was rewarded with a pained groan.

"No, don't move. Not sure where you were hit. **Orderly.** Where the hell are they?"

"Busy patchin' up the serious cases," Fred croaked with a lop-sided grin.

"Good to see your sense of humour isn't damaged," I quipped.

"Shoulder…" Fred muttered, then slipped back into oblivion.

I ran what was becoming a reasonably proficient hand over Fred. The damage he might have done to his head bothered me, but the only blood I could see was coming from his shoulder. Not necessarily good news, but not the worst news. Unable to find any other injuries for what was, I admit, a cursory examination, I deemed it acceptable to carry him to the aid post.

"Corporal." I nodded at Charlie Townsend. "Give me a hand. I'm not waiting."

Charlie and I joined hands to fashion a makeshift chair. With utmost care, and a bit of help from those in the vicinity, Fred was hefted onto the 'seat'. It was awkward because we had to keep low, the trench network was not three people wide, and Fred was lolling precariously but, by dint of shuffling sideways, we managed.

I was glad of the evening breeze when we reached the aid post.

"Shot in the shoulder. Landed on his head. As far as I can tell, no other injuries," I panted to a passing orderly, as we propped Fred against a convenient wall. He had not roused again; his lips were pinched, and his face was ashen — apart from the livid bruise forming at his hair line. Then again, everyone's face was ashen, so that was no real indicator of anything.

The poor orderlies were overwhelmed by the sheer volume of casualties. As fast as they shovelled patients onto ambulances, another batch appeared. At first glance, it seemed complete pandemonium but, while we waited for someone to help Fred, I realised it was running like a well-oiled machine.

Everyone knew their job and stuck to it rigidly. The critical cases were moved by stretcher to an ambulance, preferably one of the new motorised variety. The jolting was no less uncomfortable than a wagon, but speed mattered, and the patient would be at the Dressing Station or, if warranted, a Field Ambulance far more quickly.

Those deemed less seriously injured were assisted to the Dressing Station, which I knew to be in an old farmhouse about six hundred yards back from the trenches. Some were carried on litters; others were helped by their mates. The long line of men trudging away — shoulders slumped, gait pained — left a strange knot in my chest. It was like watching a procession of the dead.

The walking wounded would be given basic first aid here. To be honest, it didn't bear thinking about. Aside from the constant barrage of artillery, the orderlies and bearers were reduced to cleaning and dressing wounds, administering pain relief and any other medication required, under abominable conditions. It would be a miracle if anyone survived.

Funnily enough, despite this, the overriding mood was positive, almost cheery, and completely at odds with the situation. Hot cocoa, brandy, and biscuits were shared out. Men chatted while being bandaged or suffering an anti-tetanus injection. The soft chink of tin mugs clinking together as they celebrated being alive.

I allowed myself a wry grin… nowhere was the British indomitable pluck more apparent.

Five

"He needs more'an I can give 'im," the medic's voice broke my train of thought, and I refocused on the young man in front of me.

He pursed his lips, meditatively. "Hmmm, a through and through, but I reckon it's clipped 'is shoulder blade, and I don't want to risk bandagin' 'im up and sending 'im back to the line, 'specially given 'e landed on 'is 'ead. FA's best place for 'im, the DS'll be overflowing by now," referring to the Field Ambulance and Dressing Station, respectively.

I exhaled a silent sigh of relief. The FA was *almost* out of harm's way. Certainly, further from the front line than the Dressing Station. This was good and bad news. Good because Fred had a much better chance of a full recovery, bad because it implied his wound might be graver than I suspected.

The medic read me like a book.

"He'll do," he reassured. "I just prefer him to be examined where they 'ave more time. Shoulders can be tricky. Don't want to miss a fragment of bone. Also, 'e'll bear watchin' with that crack to 'is skull. Transport'll be along in a jiffy."

Which could mean anything from five minutes to five hours.

"Thank you…" I arched a questioning brow.

"Corp'ral Hughes, sir, but Archie'll do," the young man replied, a tired grin lighting his grubby features.

"Thank you, Corporal. I'll wait with Corporal Cuthbert if I am not in your way."

"As yer like, sir. Here…" Hughes twisted slightly to grab a battered mug and equally maltreated water bottle. With a dexterity born of frequency, he sloshed a large measure into the mug and handed it to me. "That'll keep the chill off."

I dipped my head gratefully, savouring the whiff of brandy, as I swallowed a gulp, coughing when the spirit hit the back of my throat. Foregoing customary address, I rasped, "Charlie?" and offered him the mug.

He echoed my gesture, then wiped the back of his hand across his mouth. "By that hit the spot, sir." He hesitated, obviously torn between staying with Fred and me, and rejoining the unit. Here was undoubtedly safer, but Charlie was not one to leave his post, and likely he was chomping at the bit to check on his mates.

"Go on, Corp'ral. Find the lads and give them an update on Cuthbert. I'll be back as soon as."

"Sir." Charlie scarpered.

"Head down," I exhorted, chuckling when he ducked his tall frame until his head was below the rim of the trenches.

We waited. Slowly, the aid station emptied, leaving only those requiring transport to the Field Ambulance… and there was a queue, systematically prioritised. The rumble of the motorised vehicles ebbed and flowed with sickening regularity, while the horse drawn wagons transported the less urgent cases.

Fred swam in and out of consciousness. I talked to him, but doubted he was aware of my presence.

At the now familiar growl of an engine, Corporal Hughes came over with a stretcher bearer and, between the three of us, we manoeuvred Fred onto the taut canvas.

Carefully, we carried Fred towards the approaching vehicle. It stopped; the driver hopped out and went around to open the flaps.

I felt my forehead furrow. I had heard more and more women were driving ambulances, supposedly to free up the men for other jobs, and wondered how they coped. It was one thing being assigned to a hospital ward, quite another risking life and limb coming right to the front line.

My innate instinct to protect the fairer sex from the atrocities we witnessed every day, warred with my awareness that women were probably far more capable than we gave them credit for. Still, it seemed a tad reckless... another opinion I intended to keep to myself.

The driver turned to greet us.

My jaw dropped.

"*Polly?*" I heard my tone rise in incredulity.

The woman looked at me properly. I watched as recognition dawned.

For what felt like an eternity, although it was less than five seconds, we stared at each other.

I swore then and will continue to swear until my dying breath, that the world tilted on its axis. I was cocooned in a bubble comprised of Polly and me as the hubbub around us receded.

"*Thad?*" her stunned exclamation shattered my trance, and the din of the war returned.

"You from the FA?" I could not help my shocked question.

"Yes," she replied somewhat distractedly, then sharply, "The Lincolnshires... why are you..." the obvious answer seemed to rob her of coherence, and her gaze slid to the stretcher. "Fred?" she husked, trying to mask her shock. "Oh no… Maisie."

"Bullet to the shoulder. Possible head injury." Corporal Hughes interjected, reciting the pertinent details, and I watched as Polly pulled professionalism over her like a cloak.

Polly nodded as he talked, her focus on Fred, who chose that moment to come around.

"P-Po*lly*?" he croaked. His shock matched mine, which, in any other circumstance, would be comical.

"Well, Corporal Cuthbert what the dickens were you doing to get yourself shot?" she quizzed gaily. "Ignoring orders, I daresay."

"Bloody hurts," he groaned.

"'Course it does. What do you expect? You took a bullet. No need to fret, it's naught but a graze, and your arm is still attached."

Fred's mouth curved slightly at Polly's brisk no-nonsense manner.

"Let's get you out of here. Thank you, Archie." She sent the orderly a warm smile and, without warning, my chest tightened.

Confused by my reaction, I ignored it. "You can manage…?" I stopped short, careful not to make it sound as though I did not trust her to get Fred to the FA.

"Thank you, Warrant Officer Jenkins, I've got this." Her blue eyes sparkled with something akin to mischief, as though she knew what was going on my head and found it amusing.

I sketched a bow and, stepped aside as Archie and the bearer slotted the stretcher into the ambulance, along with three others.

"I'll get a message to you about Fred," Polly promised as she climbed back into her seat, the door creaking shut in protest. With a wave, she was gone.

She drove off with remarkable ease given the deplorable state of the tracks. I watched the squat black vehicle until it was merely a speck on the horizon, then returned to my unit.

1st July 1916 — Field Ambulance
Polly

Dawn crept in. Through the slits in the tent, slivers of light danced across my face. I blinked and squeezed my eyelids shut, desperate for even five more minutes' sleep, knowing it was futile.

I found it hard enough getting up for our usual shift but today, it was a good two hours earlier. Wearily, I dragged myself out of my cot and woke Cilla before scurrying through my morning ritual.

"Nooooooo," I heard Cilla protest and snuggle back under the thin blanket.

I tickled her neck, making her giggle and grouse at the same time.

"Brrr… your fingers are like ice, ger'off."

I ignored her. "You know I can keep this up all day, and better me than the Dragon."

Acknowledging the truth of my words, Cilla, with marked reluctance, threw back the covers and swung her legs off the bed, shivering.

"Hop to it, I'll go and see whether there's a brew." I grinned at her disgruntled expression and, checking my uniform once more, hurried across to the, euphemistically termed, canteen. In reality, an old barn adjacent to the FA, which the army had commandeered for the purpose.

It leaked like a sieve when it rained and, occasionally, the wind whistled through the multitude of cracks with such force, we were surprised it remained upright. That said, it freed up another tent for the wounded, and the farmer who owned the the barn was glad of the extra rations we sent his way in gratitude for his generosity.

I stretched and rolled my shoulders, breathing in the cool fresh air. A welcome, albeit temporary, respite before we were bathed in sweltering summer heat. I stared up at the clear sky, the blue deepening slowly as the sun rose.

A glorious day was in the offing.

A deadly day was also in the offing.

The mood around the FA was sombre. We all knew what the next few hours would bring.

Morning prayers said and breakfast eaten, Cilla and I, along with several other nurses and orderlies, under the watchful eye of the Dragon, checked our supplies for the hundredth time.

Counted and recounted bandages and blankets. Ensured the trays of instruments were prepared as per each surgical team's preferences and stacked accordingly.

During the previous couple of days, we had scrubbed the camp from top to bottom until Matron was satisfied.

Currently, and for the first time since my arrival, we were empty of patients. Every last one had been evacuated to the Casualty Clearing Station, from where they would be transported to a base hospital. The FA was unnaturally quiet.

7:30 loomed. We knew that was when the offensive would begin.

My whole body tensed up.

We had done everything we could. There was nothing left to do except wait.

Waiting was the worst. Once the wounded started coming in, we were too busy to woolgather but, prior to the arrival of that first stretcher of the never-ending train, it was like teetering on the edge of a precipice.

"Thank you, girls," the Dragon's voice pierced my preoccupation… no bad thing. "Go on, take a quick walk around camp, I daresay none of us will get the chance shortly."

It took everything I had not to let my jaw drop. I scarcely felt Marjorie Elsey, the third member of our quartet, nudge my elbow. "Come on Polly," she muttered under her breath. "I need another cuppa before hell lands on our doorstep."

"Matron," we chorused in unison and fled.

That was the last moment of peace for what felt like an eon.

Six

2nd July 1916 — Field Ambulance
Polly

When I looked back on that day — no, it was more like two, possibly three days — it remains a blur, save one fateful moment.

It seemed as though the opening salvo of the offensive had barely been launched when the first of the wounded trickled in. In what felt like the blink of an eye, although was probably over the course of several hours, the trickle became a deluge.

With each injury came a story. A tale we had heard countless times before, and every single one boiled down to the same thing… courage against impossible odds.

The hearing never got any easier, but to stop them telling us never entered our heads; it might be the only way they could cope with the torment.

. . .

Mid-morning on the second day, I was coming out of the operating tent, my apron smeared with goodness knew what when I spotted the Dragon advancing like a winged victory. My hurried glance around for a plausible escape route was halted at the sound of my name.

Despite my undoubtedly dishevelled appearance, I patted my head, automatically, ensuring my cap was in place.

"Armstrong, you can drive an ambulance, yes?"

"Yes Matron," I replied politely, masking my confusion at her question.

"Good, Private Watkins might be talented, but he had not yet mastered the ability to drive two vehicles at the same time, and we need to use every resource to get the wounded back. No point a perfectly good vehicle sitting idle, for want of a driver."

She flapped her hand towards the private, slouched against one of the motorised ambulances, smoking while the stretchers were unloaded. He looked exhausted, and I was not surprised.

"Matron." I looked down at my clothes. It was more than a little challenging to operate an ambulance in the regulation nurses' garb, and there was a specific uniform for drivers, but I was *not* about to argue with the Dragon and started towards the vehicles.

"Armstrong."

I paused.

"You have five minutes to change."

Startled, I stared at her, momentarily nonplussed.

"Close your mouth, Armstrong, you are not a stranded cod." A wry chuckle followed me as I dashed to my tent.

Bloody hell... was she human after all?

"And no running in uniform."

Maybe not. I shook my head and concentrated on not tripping up in my haste.

I was back at the ambulance in three minutes.

"Where's Private Dixon?" I asked, referring to the absent driver, not sure I wanted to hear the answer.

Private Watkins jerked his head at the wards.

"Must've risked the canteen, can't stop throwing up." His mouth twisted in a parody of a grin, as he pushed himself off the side of the ambulance.

"Poor kid," I murmured. Aware Private Dixon was not yet twenty, I thought it might be more to do with what he had seen than what he had eaten.

"Aye, he'll be right." Watkins' tone indicating he had no sympathy for Dixon's sensitive stomach, whatever had caused it. "Not for the faint-hearted this job." He looked me up and down, doubtless assessing my sensibilities.

"Don't you fret about me, Private. This is not the first time I've driven to an aid post. You forget, I'm from Lincolnshire where we're made of stern stuff."

"Humph, remains to be seen," was his considered opinion.

I followed him along the well-worn and rutted track leading to the aid post; the ambulance lurching and reeling like a drunken lord. No wonder poor Dixon was sick. The cacophony of war, hardly noticeable at the FA was deafening so close to the front.

I steeled my nerves and kept my foot on the accelerator, glad it was not my first time navigating these abysmal roads. It did not pay to slow down until the last minute. For some reason, the faster you drove, the less potholes you hit.

Half-way there, we passed the other two vehicles returning from the aid post, acknowledging the drivers. Our timing, honed to a fine art.

I came to a halt behind Watkins and jumped down. Men appeared from every direction carrying stretchers. Leaving the engine idling, I hurried to the rear of the ambulance, pulled open the doors and turned to help load the stretchers.

Back and forth, back and forth… our trips to and from the FA formed a pattern on endless repeat. I scarcely registered whether it was day or night, as time lost all meaning. I snatched what sleep I could at the wheel — sometimes while driving, I hate to confess.

In the aftermath, I could not fathom how I had the courage to keep returning to the horror, but it was as though my senses were numbed… no bad thing.

A ceasefire was called. Forty-eight hours when all hostilities ceased. This begged the question; if they could stop killing each other for two days, could they not make it four, then a week, then a month?

Don't be silly, mentally, I smacked my forehead. *Why on earth would sense prevail?*

The abrupt silence was deafening and, curiously, almost more frightening than the racket. It was unnatural, like being lost in the fog.

While not necessarily good news, the ceasefire allowed both sides to recover any survivors along with their dead and meant a brief lull in the flood of wounded, currently all but stacked like tins of sardines outside the hospital tents.

The sun was setting, bathing the landscape in molten gold and in a clear sky turning soft purple, I could see the twinkle of the evening star.

Our respite was about to expire.

I was on the last run of the day… I hoped. Watkins was following behind me just in case, but Archie, whose lists were invariably accurate, had stated there were four left to transfer. I yearned for a proper night's sleep, stretched out in my cot, not huddled on the hard seat of the ambulance.

Reaching the rear of the trench system, I drew up, hopped out, and opened the ambulance doors. "Roll up, roll up," I carolled. "Last call for the FA, where you will be wined and dined like a prince of the realm."

I heard a dry chuckle.

I squinted through the dusk and my gaze landed on a tall soldier.

A flicker of recognition fired up the weary cogs in my brain, and they began to grind.

"*Thad?*"

A multitude of questions tumbled into my head. The only reason for Thad Jenkins… sorry, Warrant Officer Jenkins, to be at the aid post was because he or one of the Lincolnshires was wounded.

My heart skipped a beat then thundered an erratic rhythm. I closed my eyes to calm my dread. I knew the likelihood of one of our own… for want of a better description… being hurt or worse was high, that did not mean I was prepared.

Our eyes met and, in that split second between heart beats, it was as though I was caught in some half-forgotten fantasy. Instead of blood and dirt and wounded, the scene was a fairy dell complete with a rock pool, drifts of dew-drenched flowers, and misty blue trees.

Seriously, Polly, now is not *the time for daydreaming,* I instructed inwardly, shook off the idyll, and dragged my gaze from Thad's to the stretcher, registering who lay there, pale and clearly in pain.

It was Fred Cuthbert.

Shock stole my voice, then I heard myself mutter his name as my concern for Maisie reared its head. *Please, Lord,* I prayed, *I have not the strength to tell my friend her husband has copped it.*

Archie Hughes, one of my favourite orderlies, grinned; his unwavering cheerfulness a boost to tired spirits. I reckoned the day Archie stopped smiling would be the day all hope was lost.

By sheer force of will, I assumed my professional persona and listened as Archie gave me the relevant details.

"Bullet to the shoulder. Possible head injury…"

Thad waited until Archie had finished then, asked me, "You from the FA?"

I nodded absently, my attention on Fred, who opened his eyes and gawked at me.

"P-Po*lly?*" His voice was hoarse but there was no doubt as to his surprise.

"Well, Corporal Cuthbert what the dickens were you doing to get yourself shot?" I teased brightly. "Ignoring orders, I daresay."

"Bloody hurts," he grumbled.

"'Course it does. What do you expect? You took a bullet. No need to fret, it's naught but a graze, and your arm is still attached."

I was relieved to see Fred's mouth curve ever-so slightly at my deliberately crisp tone. I sounded like the Dragon, which made me want to giggle.

"Let's get you out of here. Thank you, Archie."

"You can manage…?" Thad started to say, then pressed his lips together.

"Thank you, Warrant Officer Jenkins, I've got this," I replied, keenly aware of what he was thinking. He was not alone. Most of the soldiers I came across were startled at the sight of a woman driving an ambulance, despite — so I had been given to understand — there being a reasonable number of us dotted among the various field hospitals.

He bowed, an odd gesture, which from anyone else would seem affected. From Thad… perfectly normal.

As Archie and the bearer slid the stretcher into the ambulance, along with three others, I said — ignoring the peculiar jolt demanding I whisk Thad away from the nightmare of the trenches — "I'll get a message to you about Fred."

I was rewarded with a marginal lifting of his sombre expression. Nodding, I hopped into the cab, fought the gears, and shot off with more speed than care.

One thing about this war… you had no time to think.

Seven

4th July 1916 — Field Ambulance
Polly

Everything looked exactly the same, but everything had changed. I could not put my finger on the source of this ridiculous revelation but knew it to be unequivocal.

Was it Fred? A man I knew, thought of like a brother and married to one of my best friends, currently injured and lying in a cot scant yards from me.

I ran that around my head. No, definitely not Fred. Yes, I was concerned that someone to whom I was close was hurt, but he had not caused this peculiar state of affairs.

Try as I might, the answer hovered frustratingly out of reach. Acknowledging this was getting me nowhere, I put it aside, to be revisited when I had a quiet moment… ignoring the sheer improbability of finding a 'quiet moment' in the current crisis… or the foreseeable future for that matter.

No bad thing. I had no time for introspection — that opened a whole other can of worms.

Pleased with my pragmatism, I applied myself to things I *could* deal with, and the morning flew by. Dressings removed, wounds examined, cleaned, and re-bandaged; bed baths given, bedding changed, tents aired — the list went on. Mid-afternoon, I was summoned to assist in the operating tent where I stayed until long past moonrise.

Coming out into the relative peace of the night, I broke all the rules by removing my cap and shaking out my hair, praying the Dragon wasn't lurking in the shadows waiting to pounce on unwitting nurses.

Pausing, I rolled my aching shoulders, hearing my joints pop and realign after another long day. I ought to find my bed — dawn would arrive soon enough — but, although exhausted, I felt restless. Tonight, my mind refused to quieten.

Counting the wounded in our care, I was starting to question how this war could continue. We were only one FA; there were hundreds of medical facilities stretching from the front line to the ports, and the tally of casualties being bandied about was astronomical. Surely, both sides of this dratted war must be about to run out of soldiers.

I blew a tired sigh. As the day waned, we had lost three men, despite the trenchant efforts of the surgical teams. All young, of course, whose features, despite the appalling trauma inflicted on them, serene.

In truth, their injuries were grievous. Even if we had managed to stabilise them, it was unlikely any would have survived being transferred to the clearing station.

I stepped off the duck board which connected the operating tents to the wards and marched around the edge of the camp, nodding to the odd soldier standing guard.

Swinging my arms and flexing my hands, I tried to rid myself of the fidgets, aware it was not the loss of the three soldiers which bothered me — I had seen plenty of death — it was more the notion I was becoming immune to suffering.

I no longer flinched at injuries which, in the early days, had me fighting not to scream or throw up... or both. Men, shredded by mortar shells, or bullets, or shrapnel or disfigured by burns, barely registered anymore. We patched them up and either sent them back to the trenches or to the closest CCS.

What did I say about introspection?

It seemed as though my head had scarcely touched the pillow when reveille roused us. The last notes of the bugle were still ringing in my ears as I splashed through a cursory wash and hurried to dress.

A quick glance in the tiny mirror hanging on one of the posts in our quarters told me the wreck of the Hesperus looked more presentable than yours truly.

I grimaced at my reflection, checked my bed was made to the Dragon's exacting standards, then trudged out into the dazzling morning sunlight hoping the tea was hot and the toast not burnt.

My usual chores complete, I sat with Fred for a few minutes. His case, like many others did not necessitate evacuation up the chain and once discharged, he would be granted a week's R and R, before returning to his unit.

Exploiting my rapport with the surgical team, I had

risked a stern reprimand by daring to propose Fred stay at the FA, rather than be sent to the Clearing Station, or one of the distant hospitals to recuperate. Sweetening my suggestion by reminding them, in an excruciatingly polite and circuitous fashion, that the army camp was closer. Military efficiency and all that.

Funnily enough, this was received with approval which, I suspected… sardonically… related to our proximity to the front line, rather than any concern for Fred. He was simply one soldier among hundreds, and the more promptly they could be rotated back to the trenches, the better.

Although the bullet had ripped through the fleshy part of his shoulder, chipping his shoulder blade, the majority of the damage was confined to muscle and sinew.

His tumble into the trench had resulted in a contusion the size of an apple on the side of his head, bruising, and a black eye. Monitored for concussion, Fred… grudgingly… confided to feeling groggy, nauseous, and having double vision, but the symptoms had dissipated, and he seemed to have escaped lightly.

His wound would take time to heal but heal it most certainly would — to my chagrin. I did not wish Fred hurt, but a discharge owing to injury would be a relief, to me and definitely to Maisie.

"How are you feeling?" Gently, I rested the back of my hand on the undamaged side of his forehead for a couple of seconds, pleased to note it felt cool. His pulse was perhaps a little faster than it ought to be but, given his current state, nothing concerning.

"Sore, headache to end all headaches, and like a damn fool," came his grumbled reply.

"Why a fool?"

"Shoulda had my wits about me, stayed low. Falling on my head?" He gave a lopsided grin. "Honestly. Clumsier than a new recruit."

I couldn't prevent a chuckle. "You were carrying an injured soldier, and the ceasefire was still in place. The powers that be in this damn war need to synchronise their watches," I joked.

"You're not wrong." He tried to lift his arm and hissed a pained breath. "Bloody hell."

"What part of rest up don't you understand? It's sore now but will ease soon enough. Of course, if you expect to play cricket this weekend, forget it."

"Polly…" he hesitated, started again, then stopped, seemingly lost for words. A first.

"You are not going to die, Fred, if that's what's bothering you," I said roundly. "It's just a flesh wound, and the surgeon made sure it was clean. Your temperature is normal, there's no sign of infection. You'll be back with the lads before you know it."

"No, it's not that. I just wondered…" he trailed off again, as a hint of red washed up his pale cheeks.

I frowned. What on earth was the matter? "Fred, out with it."

"Might you write to Maisie for me?" He nodded at his arm. "She needs to know, but I can't…" his features twisted in frustration.

I burst out laughing. "Is that all? Fred Cuthbert, since when were you embarrassed to ask a favour."

He rubbed his nose with his good hand. "Just such a private thing, a letter to your wife."

"Fred, I'd be happy to. I have been writing to men's wives for months. It is an honour to help even in so small a way. Now, I think you could use a kip. I'll pop back later with my notepaper."

"Thanks, Polly." His eyes were drifting closed.

"My pleasure," I murmured, made sure his blanket covered him properly, and left him to sleep.

Eight

Polly

I added my own letter to the one I wrote for Fred and, worried Maisie might panic, scribbled a quick note to Lizzie as well.

Probably unnecessary because I swear that woman has second sight. She always seemed to know when she was needed... but a little postal nudge would not go amiss.

Fred recovered quickly, helped — I'm convinced — by the unceasing troop of his fellow soldiers who called into the FA on their rotation either out to the camp or back to the line.

It was a constant source of amazement to me how many comrades of those injured snuck in a visit. I was not complaining, their enthusiastic chatter worked wonders.

A couple of days later, I was hurrying out of the operating tent on the hunt for clean aprons when I spotted the one person who had, without permission I might add, taken root in my dreams.

Thad Jenkins.

I paused and watched his purposeful stride carry him to the wards, doubtless on his way to see Fred.

I pondered the validity of an impromptu check on the patients, immediately dismissing the notion before it was half-formed. I had no excuse to be on the wards, not least because I was due back in theatre, *"forthwith,"* Staff's order rang in my head as she sent me to fetch the supplies, "better still, yesterday if you can swing it."

I swallowed a grin. Staff was as much a martinet as the Dragon but softer around the edges.

Don't get me wrong, she expected absolute dedication and woe betide you, if you slacked off, but she always made allowances if circumstance dictated and was unfailingly kind.

Operating under the metaphor that you catch more flies with honey than vinegar, her philosophy had the entire FA eating out of the palm of her hand.

Turning, and quelling the impulse to run, I walked as fast as humanly possible to the supply tent. Collecting the required aprons and, since I was there, a pile of clean sheets and cloths, I retraced my steps. Concentrating on not drop-ping my rather precarious load, I did not register the thud of approaching feet until I collided with a solid mass.

Startled, I tottered, feeling the pristine stack start to slide out of my grasp. "Nooooooo," I wailed, executing a wild jig to prevent everything from slithering onto the dusty ground.

A hand steadied me and righted the load. "Forgive me, Nurse. I was lost in thought and did not see you there."

I knew that voice.

Thad.

Peering over the tower of material, I blew at the stray

lock of hair which had decided, of course, to unwind right at that moment and fall into my eyes… *typical.*

"It was my fault. I cannot see over this lot." I was unable, for the life of me, to prevent traitorous heat from stealing up my cheeks.

"Permit me."

Before I could demur, let alone stop him, Thad had taken the whole bundle.

"I… errr…" Corralling my recalcitrant brain, I smiled shyly. "Much appreciated."

"My pleasure. Now, where are you taking these?"

"Just over there." I pointed at the cluster of canvas which made up our operating theatres.

"How are you?" Thad asked after a few seconds of silence.

"I'm fine, thank you," I replied — a mite primly, it cannot be denied — and, without thinking, reciprocated in kind. "You?" then clapped a hand over my mouth. "Oh, I am sorry, that was a stupid question. I imagine you are exhausted, hungry, frustrated, battle weary, and desperate to go home."

A soft chuckle reached me.

"All of the above. Yet my spirits have experienced a lift."

There was something in his tone. I shot him a suspicious glance. *Was he teasing me?* His expression was unreadable, but he caught my gaze and, as we reached the tent, twisted to face me.

Without elaborating, he handed over my aprons, sheets, and cloths. "Take care, Polly." He dipped another of those gentlemanly bows and walked away.

I stared at Thad's retreating figure. Almost out of sight, he glanced over his shoulder and raised his hand. That same sensation — the one which had left me breathless at the aid post — returned with a vengeance. "Oh, for the luxury of time," I muttered, not really sure what I meant, while realising I did not have any.

Gathering my composure, I legged it.

July 1916 — Field Ambulance
Thad

I knew bumping into Polly Armstrong while visiting Fred was not beyond the realms of possibility, but the encounter caught me off guard. I had yet to equate this competent young nurse with the Polly of my recall.

Back home, we rarely crossed paths. Yes, we both lived in Nettleby, but I'm a good decade older than she, and we had few mutual friends; our only real connection was through Joe Elliott and Fred Cuthbert.

That the driver who hopped down from the ambulance at the aid post, all capable and reassuring in the midst of chaos, turned out not only to be a woman but also someone from home came as a shock. Both firsts — and no, I do not object to women doing the same jobs as men, but seeing one in the thick of it, so to speak was… unexpected.

Frustratingly… and the last thing I needed when my focus ought to be elsewhere… her heart-shaped face, sparkling blue eyes, and glossy hair in that glorious dark-blonde shade reminiscent of butterscotch, had taken up residence in my head.

During my walk back to camp, where I had two more days of R & R, my mind devised reasons — ranging from the sublime to the ridiculous — to come back to the FA.

By the time I reached my temporary accommodation, I acknowledged defeat. Fred was due to be discharged and, given the rest of my regiment was hale and hearty, I had no plausible excuse to pay a call.

Perched on the edge of the cot, I let my thoughts roam. I

never imagined experiencing the same depth of feeling for another woman as I had for Sylvia, but those two brief encounters with Polly had kindled a flicker of something I believed long dead.

I needed to be careful, though. We were living in fraught times where life was tenuous, and senses heightened. It would not behove me to act on impulse if my emotions were triggered by circumstance rather than genuine affection.

I shook my head at such pompous rationalisation. In truth, I doubted Polly saw me as anyone other than Joe's cousin, ignoring the curious pinching in my chest *that* particular notion engendered.

Get a grip, Thad Jenkins, I instructed sternly and, shoving aside what was likely fantasy on my part, went to see what the canteen was offering in the guise of food.

Nine

Thad

Back at the front, there was no time for soul-searching, we had more than enough to do defending the trenches between Foncquevillers and Berles-au-Bois.

Vague glimmers of romance, however ephemeral, might soothe a person to sleep at night — if sleep was a blessing we could indulge in — might even act as a spur when facing danger, but could not be allowed to distract.

I had the semblance of a routine. In general, I wrote reports, discussed strategy, boosted morale, and avoided enemy fire… not necessarily in that order.

Fred had returned but, in spite of his irrepressibly cheerful disposition, I suspected his shoulder plagued him. I noticed an occasional wince when he raised his rifle, or if someone jarred his arm in passing. I had no mind to mention it but it bore monitoring.

My desire to get him sent home out of harm's way, on medical grounds, vied with my desire to keep him here where his dogged optimism was contagious. Fred possessed the uncanny ability to raise his comrades' spirits with nothing more than a wise-crack or irreverent comment... usually disparaging the Hun.

It was a gift, one for which I was eternally grateful, and would be a tough act to do without... or follow.

Mind, if Fred's injury prevented him from carrying out his duties, the decision was out of my hands. I just prayed it would not come to that. In the meantime, I kept an eye on him and, as unobtrusively as possible, lightened his load.

One bright spot amongst the carnage was when those of the 1/5th Lincolnshires responsible for recovering casualties during the ceasefire after Gommecourt were awarded the Military Medal for bravery. It was a bitter-sweet commendation, given the number of casualties, but one wholeheartedly deserved.

The other bright spot was Polly. Whenever I rotated out, instead of joining in the organised sporting competitions, I found myself trekking the mile or so to the Field Ambulance. Clearly, prudence was also rotating out, especially as I had no idea when Polly was on shift.

I expected to receive a polite rebuff of my, frankly, diffident advances, surprised when Polly's reaction was the exact opposite. Her sunny greeting eased my qualms, and although the first time I plucked up the courage to 'drop by', she only had fifteen minutes to spare, it was worth the walk in the hot sun.

It became a delightful, if sporadic, habit.

Unsure about the protocol, and determined not to get Polly into trouble, I requested an interview with Matron who interrogated me in a manner the enemy could not have bettered but saw fit to grant her approval.

I think my rank might have been the deciding factor. Apparently, according to her… and I paraphrase… sergeants and above were not swayed by disreputable urges. *Little did she know… but I wasn't arguing.*

She studied me for an excruciatingly long moment, presumably assessing my integrity. Whatever she saw satisfied her. "You are consenting adults, and Armstrong has not shown any inclination to be flighty. As long as you do not interfere with her duties, her free time is her own."

Dismissed with a regal wave of her hand, I almost ran out of her office, straight into Polly.

"Oh, fancy meeting you here." Her welcoming smile doing funny things to my insides, which was both tantalising and terrifying.

"I happened to be passing." I swept a bow. "Are you free or…" I said, mentally kicking myself for the thinly disguised hope in my voice.

"If you can wait ten minutes, I have the rest of the evening," she replied.

"Perfect. I shall loiter in the canteen."

Good as her word, Polly joined me ten minutes later and, although still in uniform, had shed her apron and cap, making her look quite different.

Nothing is sacred or private in the army, and the slightest whiff of gossip is seized with relish. As we wove around the tables, one or two of her colleagues, putting two and two together and making ten, tossed ribald remarks our way.

"Give over, Warrant Officer Jenkins is just a friend from

home," Polly retaliated good-humouredly, but muttered, "Come on, how about we fill our plates then find somewhere less public and have a picnic?"

Ignoring the dip in my ego at being referred to as 'just a friend', I nodded my agreement. Shortly thereafter, we were sitting on the grass near the banks of the stream which skirted one corner of the FA with a merry gurgle.

"Sorry about them." She jerked her head towards the canteen. "They don't mean any harm."

"Nothing to apologise for. I am surprised only a couple of them felt the need share their opinion." While my choice of words was, perhaps, overly formal, I took pains to sound amused rather than affronted.

"Not enough fodder to keep them occupied," she huffed resignedly. "I daresay I'll be the topic of conversation for days."

"Would you prefer I did not visit?" I ventured.

"Why the dickens would you think that?"

I opened my palms in an 'isn't it obvious' gesture.

She wagged a finger. "Get away with you. My life is my life, if what I choose to do with it keeps other people guessing, all the better. Now, eat."

Never at a loss for topics, we chatted about life the universe and everything, while staunching our appetites. As someone used to minimal variety, the fare was quite the feast. I had heard rumours about food shortages, but if they were true, the kitchen staff here had not received the memo.

Swallowing the last mouthful, I got to my feet to rinse my fingers in the stream.

Turning to retrace my steps, I stopped dead.

My brain was swamped with lines from assorted poems, learnt as a child and promptly forgotten — no self-respecting young lad cares for flowery stanzas. Every single one of them surged to the forefront of my mind.

Reclining on her elbows, Polly was silhouetted in the golden light of the early evening sun. Minute insects, swarming in the balmy air, danced above her like an iridescent aura. Even her hair seemed to glow; the coronet of wheat-hued curls resembling a halo. For a moment, she did not look real; an illusion conjured up by exhaustion and wayward memory.

"Thad?"

Her puzzled question penetrated my reverie. I came back to earth, back to the dry ground, the babbling brook, and the most beautiful woman I have ever seen... and yes, that included Sylvia. *Well, buggeration.*

"Forgive me, my mind was elsewhere."

She canted her head to study my face, her shrewd blue gaze reading more than I realised. "With Sylvia?"

My jaw dropped. "How did you..."

"I know how much she meant to you and that, as far as I am aware, I am the first woman you have court—" she hesitated, a becoming pink warming her cheeks, "shared dinner with since you lost her."

I sank onto the grass and took her hand. Turning it over, I traced my finger over her palm. "Yes, you are, and although Sylvia featured in my thoughts, she was not the focus of them."

Polly did not avert her eyes, but I felt a faint tremor run through her fingers and squeezed them gently.

"I know we are in the middle of a war, that life is fleeting, and that we barely know each other, but I believe there is a spark between us, one which is worth nurturing to see whether it will ignite."

My old-fashioned turn of phrase was at odds with our circumstances, yet I felt it appropriate. Neither did I know how else to enunciate my attraction without sounding like a blithering idiot.

"Th-Thad," she stammered, her gaze swinging between my face and our joined hands.

"Polly," I countered gently.

Her fingers curled round mine, as she sat up. Still holding hands, we got to our feet.

I honestly wondered whether the world was holding its breath.

I grazed her nose with my lips. Her skin was cool, soft.

There were rules about courtship, and I was about to flout them all with a gesture I deemed entirely justified by the astonishment of revelation and those damn poems. Sliding one arm around Polly, I drew her against my body and kissed her.

I felt rather than heard her sigh as she melted into my arms. The sensation was sublime.

Conscious of our surroundings, I broke the kiss almost before it had begun and, lifting my head, saw Polly's mouth curve into a mischievous smile.

"Well, that is not going to curb their tongues, is it?"

Ten

Polly

August blazed into September. The summer heat refusing to relinquish its grip as the fighting ebbed and flowed like some grotesque dance and, although the gains seemed minimal, the list of casualties was not.

Whatever the genesis of this war, you would imagine by now, that the Hun… exercising the brains they were born with… had registered the fact, the allies were never going to surrender, rendering the whole thing futile. Then, if the powers that be could simply agree to disagree, we could all go home.

Good grief, Polly… what are you thinking? I remonstrated to myself. *Never let common sense get in the way of fragile egos.*

My budding romance — if one could call our infrequent rendezvous a romance — with Thad did much to keep the horrors of war at bay. We took long walks, or cycled into the local town, or explored the miraculously unravaged countryside and, for those brief interludes, pretended we were any other courting couple.

It was a constant source of astonishment to me that, a few short miles from the front line, life — outwardly, at least — continued as though naught was amiss. That there was not a bloody conflict raging just beyond their doorstep, and that the rumble punctuating the tranquillity was not the growl of distant thunder but artillery.

Notwithstanding this heartbreakingly stark contrast, the respite was bliss, and we savoured every golden opportunity.

The whole of the FA knew of our courtship but, funnily enough, after an initial gentle ribbing, no one teased me. I supposed this was because everyone was keenly aware that tomorrow was not guaranteed, and none of them wanted to spoil the precious moments Thad and I were able to share. A generosity of spirit which warmed my soul.

It was a time for discovery… of each other, more so than the neighbourhood. Our attraction might be heartfelt but was it enduring? Basking in each other's company was marvellous, but not sufficient to sustain a lifetime of trials and tribulations, highs and lows, joys and sorrows.

Life at the front came with a unique set of challenges, designed to test even the most resolute. Whatever happened, we would carry the burden of this war long after peace was declared… if it was ever declared.

Our indelible connection — forged during an impromptu picnic, and blossoming while we had fun, while relaxing away from the everyday grind — was cemented during serious discussions about our deepest fears and darkest moments. When we shared stories no one should have to share, when I cried on Thad's shoulder about losing a patient, when he vented his frustrations about the futility of war; when we listened, really listened to each other with empathy and understanding.

We had not uttered the words customarily professed to seal a relationship. I was not sure either of us was ready to articulate the depth of our devotion, but it was imbued into every dizzying kiss, every smile, every touch.

For now, that was enough.

Finally, the days began to cool and, as autumn cloaked the land in its jewel-like brilliance, I was driving ambulances more than assisting with operations.

I concede it was a tough assignment, navigating the oft hairy roads and stray mortars. The shifts were longer; I still had ward duty, and was on call every night, but it trumped the stuffy confines of the operating tent.

My bunk mates thought me mad.

"I cannot fathom what there is to like about bumping over those god-awful roads to fetch the wounded from right next to the danger zone," Cilla observed while we were having tea one afternoon.

"It's not safe," Iris chimed in. "They're bloody death traps. What if you were to roll or, worse, get blown up?" She pinned me with a wide-eyed stare.

"I'm careful, and at least I get to spend the day in the fresh air."

"And what do you call this?" Cilla flapped a hand at the view outside the canteen. "Scotch mist? How much fresh air do you need? Anyway, it's too cold to be out in the elements, and Iris is right, it's risky driving on your own, especially at night. What if you took a wrong turn and ended up in no-man's land, or worse..." her voice dropped to a theatrical whisper, "...enemy territory?"

I burst out laughing at her dramatic tone. "I'm not a complete idiot, Cilla," seeing her affronted expression, I gave her a quick hug, "but bless you for worrying about me." Including Iris in my thanks.

"'Course," She shot me an impish grin. "We have enough to do without picking up your chores as well, right Iris?"

"Right." Iris chuckled. "You can wash your own bedpans."

Duty called, and our light-hearted banter was curtailed and forgotten… almost.

November 1916 — Foncquevillers
Thad

The welcome cool and occasional dawn frosts of autumn with accompanying mantle of glorious colour, seemed to come and go in the blink of an eye. Erased by days of incessant rain, transforming the parched earth into a sea of mud, and saturating the sunbaked trench network, then — as temperatures plummeted — froze.

You might presume a landscape veiled in glistening white snow, the smattering of trees and shrubs which had withstood the indiscriminate destruction, festooned with shimmering crystal-like icicles was a sight to behold.

Not for us.

Almost overnight, the ground went from glutinous to granite — iron would have been more malleable — and any attempt to extend or dig new trenches was nigh on impossible, as was keeping warm. The cold became a far greater foe than the enemy, whole regiments struck down by the assorted seasonal maladies cutting an insidious swathe through the troops.

The damp and all-pervading chill proved to be the final

straw for Fred. The weakness in his shoulder hampered his ability to wield his weapon.

He hid it well, but I noticed him struggling with even the lightest task. The set of his jaw, the way he tensed up before lifting anything, the odd spasm when he moved without thinking, the rigid cast to his face, and the not quite suppressed hiss of discomfort.

It could not continue.

Reluctantly, I petitioned the medical board, detailing the case and, upon their reply, summoned Fred to my dugout.

"Corporal Cuthbert, while I applaud your loyalty and diligence, you are now risking more than your own life. Much as I would like to keep you here, for the morale of the unit if nothing else, I cannot have an incapacitated soldier under my command."

He opened his mouth to refute my assertion.

"No." I spoke before he could get a word in. "There is no argument you can make to change my decision. All it requires is the board's approval. I'm sorry, but if they agree with my recommendation, I have no alternative but to discharge you from service."

I smothered a laugh at Fred's stunned expression, and softened my tone, appealing to him as a friend not his superior officer.

"Fred, you must see you cannot go on like this. You think I'm unaware of the pain you're in? To say nothing of the fact, you're an appalling shot when you use your left arm. Won't need the Germans to finish us off, we'll end up killed by friendly fire."

At my dry chuckle, he looked sheepish. "Didn't think it was that obvious."

"A blind man could see what you are trying to conceal. Now, get your things and see whether you can cadge a lift to the FA. The surgeon who patched you up will need to examine you, then, I daresay it'll be back to camp until formalities are concluded."

We chatted briefly, then I clapped him on his good shoulder. "I'll miss you Fred, but I'm glad you're getting out of here…" I did not feel it pertinent to add that he was one of the lucky ones. "Safe journey home. Give my best to Nettleby."

I watched him trudge back along the trench to his mates. I knew Fred felt as though he was abandoning us, relieved to see Harry Alderton and Charlie Townsend disabuse him of that nonsensical notion — he would believe them before he believed me — their pleasure at his news, instant and unfeigned.

An hour later, loaded down with hurriedly scrawled letters from all and sundry, he was gone.

Fred was only one person, a tiny cog in a huge wheel yet, as I had anticipated, his departure left a hole the size of a bomb crater.

It took all I had not to drop everything and run hell for leather to the FA and Polly.

Eleven

November 1916 — Field Ambulance
Polly

I had never known cold like it and the winters in Nettleby could be harsh. The bitter wind whistled around the tents on a malicious crusade to pinpoint the slightest chink in the canvas with its icy fingers. Trying to keep the patients warm, much less ourselves, was a constant duel against the elements.

Thus far, the elements were winning.

There were not enough blankets, enough fuel for the stoves, enough mittens, scarves, or hats. Some of the patients were wearing several pairs of pyjamas to stave off the chill.

Our sleeping quarters sported a stove but to leave it smouldering in order to maintain some vestige of heat when the tent was unoccupied wasted our rapidly diminishing supply of wood. Even lit, it took forever to warm the inadequately insulated tent.

To preserve our resources, everyone gravitated to where four or more people were congregated, and if space was at a premium in the canteen, you tried the operating tents because, gruesome as it sounds, blood is warmer than the air.

No doubt outsiders would be galled at how many people volunteered to 'observe' when the surgeons were dealing with open wounds. None of us felt we were being disrespectful. Lumps of ice cannot save lives.

The weather also played havoc with the ambulances. We ensured the horses had a weather-proof stable, plenty of hay, and proper rugs, while those of us who could knit made little protectors for their poor ears.

Although the wagons fared better than the motorised vehicles because there was no engine to service, the weeks of rain followed by arctic temperatures warped the wooden frames and the wheels, requiring constant repair and reinforcement.

The motorised vehicles had to be maintained to the highest standard at all times. We could not risk a dead battery, thickening of engine oil or transmission fluid, or ice build-up in the fuel tank.

I was leaning over the engine of one of the ambulances, checking the oil when I heard someone call my name.

"Polly."

I hopped down to see Fred walking towards me. I frowned, momentarily nonplussed. *What was he doing here?* Then I spotted the papers in his hand and recalled overhearing a comment about one of the Lincolnshires being sent home.

"Wrawby bound?" I raised a brow, quashing an unexpected bout of homesickness.

"For my sins," he joked. "Seems I've become a liability to the unit." His shrug accompanied by a grimace.

His smile slipped slightly.

I nudged him with my elbow. "Is that what they said?"

"Not in so many words…"

"Corporal Cuthbert, stop that right there. You know fine well, Thad Jenkins would not recommend a discharge unless he had no alternative," I contradicted with a snort. "Be glad you are getting out of here. There's many won't be as fortunate."

"I know, I'm not ungrateful, it's just…" he stopped, and I knew what bothered him. Same as bothered all those who got sent home on medical grounds, but whose wounds were not obvious. The notion they were somehow shirking their duty, abandoning their mates, abandoning King and Country, combined with the prospect of being judged as cowards by busybodies back home.

"What did the doc say?"

He shot me a rueful grin. "What do you reckon?"

I tapped my chin contemplatively. "Probably that there was always the chance the injury could become debilitating, hmmm… almost certainly exacerbated by repetitive tasks, like digging trenches or firing a rifle, oh, and the execrable weather we are enjoying. Am I close?"

Fred's half-smile morphed into a grudging chuckle. "Nail on the head."

"So, how about instead of worrying about everyone else, you focus on the upside. You are going home, back to Maisie, back to the most wonderful corner of the world. Embrace it. If not for yourself, for all those who didn't make it."

"When did you get so wise?" His tone was gently teasing.

I stuck out my tongue; a childish gesture but one which lightened a conversation threatening to become emotional.

With comical roll of his eyes, he changed the subject. "How are you?"

"I'm fine, Fred." My reply did not sound particularly convincing. Covering, I rubbed my grubby hands on an old rag tucked in my pocket and kicked a wheel. "I spend more time fixing these bloody ambulances than driving them."

We chatted for a few more minutes, then Fred blew a weighty breath.

"I have to go. Please take care, Polly," he implored. "It's a dangerous business…"

"Don't say it, Fred," I interrupted. "It's bad luck. Give Maisie and Lizzie my love. Safe travels." I rummaged under the cloth and fished out two crumpled letters. "I daresay you've already got a great pile, but will these fit? I've been carrying them around," I clarified, blushing at their sorry state.

He grinned his assent. We hesitated, awkwardly.

I blinked back a rush of tears, gave him a fierce hug, and hurried away, muttering, "Bye, Fred."

While chuffed Fred was escaping this hell, I did not think I had the strength to watch him leave.

December 1916 — Foncquevillers
Polly

The atrocious weather had little effect on the war, save the men had to deal with frostbite on top of everything else, leaving me no time to dwell on Fred's departure.

The Lincolnshires were part of the division holding the

line between Foncquevillers and Berles-au-Bois, furnishing us with a steady stream of casualties.

I had driven the ambulance to and from the front line so frequently, I could probably negotiate the route blindfolded. Cilla continued to question my sanity and, occasionally, I worried about possible hazards but, without us, soldiers died and *that* I could not countenance.

So, we persevered.

One gloomy afternoon in early December, the radio crackled with a request to collect a couple of soldiers — who required more care than the limited facility could provide — from the ruined farmhouse, currently acting as a Dressing Station.

Rugged up to the nines against the frigid air, I was about to set off when Private Watkins rolled up.

Leaning out of his window, he jerked his thumb upwards and shouted, "Watch the sky, Polly. More snow on the way."

"Thanks, Sid," I called back… we had been on first name terms for months, saving formal address when in the company of officialdom. "Bad out there?" I was referring to the wounded not the weather.

"Seen worse," came his habitually casual reply.

I grinned and accelerated, taking care not to skid the wheels on the icy ground. Sending Sid a quick wave, I turned onto the pitted road.

Gripping the steering wheel, I tried to bounce with the jolts rather than brace against them. The ambulance careened wildly as I swerved this way and that, up and down hillocks of drifting snow, cursing up a storm. *Good job my mother was hundreds of miles away.*

On a good day, the journey to the dressing station took around fifteen minutes.

Today was not a good day.

The ruts left by Sid's ambulance were difficult to follow and most of the landmarks normally used as a guide were buried under deep snow. *So much for doing this route blindfolded.*

My eyes glued to the windscreen, I slowed the vehicle. A set of tracks veered off to the right. That would take me to the aid post, meaning I was pretty close to the dressing station. Straight ahead for about a hundred yards, then left and follow the drive to the farmyard.

Large white flakes began to float down from the leaden clouds. "Not yet," I grumbled to the heavens. "Let me get home."

I was concentrating so hard on the road, I overshot the gateway, "Bloody, bugger, and sod. Not the time for mistakes, Armstrong."

Huffing an aggrieved sigh, I trundled along a little further seeking somewhere to turn the ambulance.

"Hah," I exclaimed gleefully, spying a suitable gap in the hedge, and executed a reasonably efficient three point... in this case more like eight point... manoeuvre. Giddy with relief, I slithered back on course and crept forward keeping an eye out for the lane.

The snow was getting heavier. *Dammit.* Urgency spurred me on, and I increased my speed.

I could see the gate.

Yes!

Braking, I steered the ambulance towards the entrance to the farm.

I heard a peculiarly piercing whine. *Was it the wind?* I stared at the wintry landscape. The trees were not moving. *What then?*

The world exploded.

Twelve

Polly

T he ambulance, with me inside, became airborne before plunging back to earth with a bone-jarring crunch.

The vehicle pitched to one side alarmingly and, despite quivering like barely set jelly, I leant the other way, yanking the steering wheel with all my strength in a, plainly pointless, attempt to force it back onto all four tyres.

Terrifying scenarios raced through my head, and I bit down on a scream of unadulterated panic as momentum won the battle of wills.

With a dreadful squeal of grinding metal, snapping of wood, and splintering of glass, the ambulance listed too far and toppled into a hedge.

I heard the creak of the heavy vehicle settling, wedging itself into the foliage, then nothing as darkness consumed me.

When I opened my eyes, nothing had changed and, I

guessed, given I seemed reasonably warm and dry, my descent into oblivion had been blessedly brief. I was lying in a twisted heap, tangled around steering wheel, gear lever and pedals, liberally sprinkled in slivers of shattered windscreen.

Had I been hit by a mortar? Was it an ambush? Cilla's grim prediction came back to me in the greying light of the late afternoon.

Flurries of snow wafted through the gaping hole, adding to my discomfort.

The absolute silence unnerved me more than I would ever admit.

Disorientated and winded, I blinked and gulped one… two… three deep breaths, wondering why I couldn't hear the growl of the engine.

You have to get out, Polly. Trembling, I began to extricate myself from the confusion that was once the cab. Cold fingers thwarted my efforts but, slowly, I hauled my aching body out through the torn canvas canopy and managed not to fall off the upended chassis.

Brushing off the assorted debris clinging to my clothes and hair, I realised my head was throbbing. Pressing a hand to my temple, I discerned a bump and sticky wetness. I checked my palm — it was smeared with blood. *Well, isn't this just the icing on the cake.*

Wearily, I reached into the back of the ambulance and snagged the handle of my satchel, which contained a first aid kit.

I patted the distorted frame of the vehicle. "Sorry old girl, I'll don't think a bandage is going to cut it." Startled to register my words were almost inaudible.

I frowned, then stopped because the creasing of my forehead hurt. Again, I spoke aloud… the same result. *Was I deaf?* I yawned trying to make my ears pop, but nothing happened.

Pulling my long winter coat around me, and glad I was wearing several layers of clothes, I took stock.

I had no clue what had tossed the ambulance into the air so violently but did not deem it prudent to wait to find out. I had to get to the dressing station.

A man materialised out of the whirling snow.

Presuming him to be someone from the farm come to check on who was causing such a ruckus, I smiled, and gesticulated towards the mangled ambulance. "Accident." My words muffled.

The man did not reply. Aiming his rifle at me, he advanced with determination.

Something was not right, but my head was spinning, the ground kept undulating, and my senses were not functioning at full capacity.

"Sich beeilen," he barked and motioned at the road with his weapon.

Never was I more grateful to have learnt rudimentary German. He was instructing me to get a move on.

"Sorry, I can't. I'm supposed to be picking up wounded soldiers." I have no idea what prompted my protest. Plainly, my brain had yet to catch up with my eyes.

He reiterated the order and jabbed at me with the muzzle of the rifle.

Finally, I understood.

He was not from the dressing station.

He was a German soldier, and I was at his mercy.

I just had to get the cherry on the top.

Unbeknownst to me, my unwitting leave of absence was about to precipitate a rescue mission. Much, *much* later when informed of the immediate and diligent response, the good-will of my friends and colleagues reduced me to tears.

I was only small fish in a gargantuan sea, and every single person who helped had better things to do than waste their time searching for me… yet, without thought of their own safety, they downed tools and pitched in.

Advanced Dressing Station
Ruined Farmhouse
Foncquevillers
Bob Carmichael - Doctor

The muffled *whump* barely warranted comment among our little crew busy in the old farmhouse. We were more concerned with keeping men alive, than worrying about the odd stray mortar. Along with one of my assistants, Jim Travers, we prepared two soldiers for transfer.

"Ambulance'll be here in a jiffy," I reassured them, wrapping another blanket around the soldier lying on the stretcher closest to me.

"Should've been 'ere be now," Jim ruminated out loud.

"Probably coming up the drive as we speak." I glanced out of the window. "Mind, need to get a spurt on or they'll be snowed in."

The moments ticked by with no sound of an approaching engine… the drone of an ambulance was unmistakeable… and no cheerful greeting from the driver, all of whom were familiar to the staff manning the dressing station.

Seemingly, the distant boom of munitions detonating had given Jim an odd sense of foreboding. "Do you s'pose…" he hesitated. "Nah, forget it."

"What?" I pressed.

"That explosion…" Jim walked to the door, opened it, and peered into the veil of soft whiteness. "The ambulance should be here by now."

I joined him and we stared along the tree-lined drive. Nothing.

"Now you've got me worried," I grumbled.

"No harm in checking." He grinned as he shrugged into his heavy coat. "I'll be back."

Grabbing a torch, he switched it on, the beam bobbing on the snow-covered ground.

Shortly thereafter, the door banged open and Jim burst in bringing with him a glacial draft and an eddy of snow. All of us in the spartan room stopped what we were doing to look at him.

"When I got to the gate, there was neither hide nor hair of the ambulance. I shone the torch right round, but all I saw were trees. I didn't want to hang about, it's bloody freezing out there, but then I spotted something weird in the hedge and went to investigate." He paused.

It was like waiting for the punchline of a really bad joke.

With no small amount of drama, he declared, "Ambulance is on its side. No sign of the driver. We need to radio the FA."

"Whoa, steady on, lad. Say that again," I said, against a background of indrawn breaths. It wasn't so much that I didn't hear Jack, it was that I did not quite believe my ears.

Nodding at the radio operator who relayed the information verbatim, Jim repeated himself.

The voice at the other end, after checking the veracity of the transmission, confirmed the identity of the driver and that a search party would be dispatched to the farmhouse as soon as feasible.

"I doubt it'll be tonight," I said, aware how easily people could take a wrong turn in this weather.

"We can't stand about here and do nothing." Jim had his hand on the door. "It's Polly, not some trained soldier. She could be injured or worse."

"And you could get lost in this blizzard," I replied, very reasonably I thought.

"I have to try."

A couple of others offered to help, and the trio vanished into the twilight.

"Well, this is a pretty kettle of fish," I said to one of the soldiers on the stretchers. "Might as well make a brew."

Field Ambulance
Private Watkins

I stared at the Dragon in shock. "Beggin' yer pardon, Matron, but what did you just say?"

"It appears, Nurse Armstrong has met with some kind of accident. She is missing and the ambulance is upside down in a hedge. Never mind that this weather will hamper any search party, there are two soldiers who cannot be left at the DS another night. Are you up to it?"

Was I up to it? Sheesh what a question. "Of course, Matron. Me ambulance is ready to go. May I take Private Dixon. Just in case?"

Matron granted permission, and I was about to dash off when a thought struck me. "What about Warrant Officer Jenkins?"

"He's not missing, Watkins."

"No, but he and Po... Nurse Armstrong are stepping out.

What if…" I stopped, unwilling to infringe some unknown regulation, or blurt out what worried me.

I watched as the Dragon weighed up my concerns. "Leave that with me. If I think the WO needs advising, I shall ensure he is. Chances are the lass'll be found before you get there. No sense worrying people unnecessarily."

Conceding the logic behind matron's decision, I crossed my fingers that she was correct.

Within ten minutes, Private Dixon in the passenger seat, I shot out of the motor pool to be swallowed up into the darkness.

It was going to be a long night.

Thirteen

Shed — Middle of Nowhere
Polly

Head aching and heart pounding, certain I was going to feel a bullet slice through me with every footfall, I trudged through the deepening snow barely a step ahead of the German soldier.

While the haziness clouding my mind had yet to dissipate, I was *compos mentis* enough to recognise I was in a bit of a pickle.

How had he crossed the front line? Why?

Was he part of a larger unit preparing an assault? No, that did not make sense. If that was the case, surely, he would have shot me on sight.

Had he become separated from his regiment somehow? That seemed more plausible, but begged the question as to why he opted to risk discovery by approaching the aid station, blowing up an ambulance, and kidnapping me?

Another more sinister motive badgered me — sporadic warnings about what might befall a nurse if she was caught by an enemy soldier — but I refused to let it take root. What were the chances this German knew a woman was driving the ambulance? Next to zero… let alone that he might well have killed me in the blast.

No answers were forthcoming but trying to deduce his reasoning helped combat the dread clawing at me. A small, hut-like structure loomed up at the edge of the road and he directed me towards it.

My teeth were chattering now — nothing to do with the frigid temperatures or the snow trickling down the back of my neck.

I bit my lips to stop them from trembling and instructed myself not to cry. *You are British, Polly, your stiff upper lip is not about to crumble.* Mustering up my swiftly evaporating courage, I straightened my shoulders. No way was I going to let him see me cower or beg for my life.

The muzzle of his rifle jabbed me, and I stumbled to my knees. To my surprise, I felt a hand hook under my elbow and lift me upright.

Unable to help myself, I braved a glance at my captor.

His face betrayed nothing of his intent, but he motioned to the building with his weapon. "Inside," he barked in English, his tone brooking no argument.

As though I was in any position to dissent.

There was no light to alleviate the obscurity, which did not stop me from squinting. I heard the door scrape shut and waited for the click of the rifle being cocked… or worse.

It never came.

Instead, a match was struck and the wick on a candle flickered to life. The German held it aloft, and I was able to pick out the interior of what I surmised to be a shed or outhouse.

Ramshackle was the politest description I could come up with, although, *praise be*, the roof was intact.

As my eyes adjusted to the dimness, I let out a startled squeak. The subdued glimmer illuminated a hump of clothes in a corner, next to which sat another man wearing the same uniform as my abductor.

Baffled, I turned to the German standing like a silent sentinel behind me.

I opened my palms in the universal gesture for *what the dickens?*

In halting and very broken English accompanied by an elaborate and reasonably easy to decipher mime, I established that the huddle was actually a badly wounded soldier, and they wanted me to treat him. The second man nodded and smiled his approval. The man under the covers did not move.

Slack jawed, I gaped; temporarily robbed of breath… and coherence. "I do not have the medical equipment to help him," I said, then scrabbled about my brain and repeated it in hesitant German, praying my recall was correct and I had not just insulted them.

"Help you must. Friends, me, him." He gestured between the three of them and his voice wobbled.

I looked at him. Really looked at him. Under the badly fitting helmet, his features were pinched, and his eyes haunted. He was scarcely more than a kid.

My objection died on my lips. *What choice did I have anyway?*

"I cannot promise. My bag has minimal equipment. Why oh, why did you blow up the ambulance? Far easier to stand in front of it with your gun aimed at me." I tutted in exasperation.

The soldier stared at me, his baffled expression telling me, my reproof had sailed right over his head.

"Too much English," I groused under my breath, and attempted to translate. Some of it must have been intelligible because, in spite of the shadows, I caught the red stain stealing up his pale cheeks.

Too late now. Shaking my head, I crossed the dirty floor to the corner. "Light," I demanded. "Licht!"

The glow grew brighter as the soldier carried the candle closer.

Holding my breath, I peeled back the covers which turned out to be two coats and an old sack.

I heard a pained groan from the man who lay on his side bent almost double.

"I cannot examine him like this," I muttered half to myself.

Seemingly, the second soldier had a grasp of English. He rested a hand on my arm, then shook his comrade's shoulder and, speaking gently in his own language, coaxed the barely conscious man onto his back.

The smell was enough for me to know this man was beyond my help. He was beyond anyone's help. I studied him with an experienced eye, ticking off a list in my head.

Waxy, sallow skin.

Hollow cheeks.

Bruised eyes.

Dry, chapped lips.

Harsh, shallow breathing.

Gently, I unbuttoned what was left of his grey tunic, most of it in tatters by whatever had struck him.

"When?" I looked at the first soldier. "Wann?"

He shrugged. "Vier Tage."

Four days… the man had some fight in him.

"Wei?" How.

He put his palms together, then lifted his arms and his hands jerked out and up in a convulsive movement. Then he ducked and clutched his stomach. I took this to mean he was injured by some kind of incendiary device. That explained the shredded material.

Digging through my satchel, I found a pair of scissors and, carefully, cut away the layers of clothes to expose his upper body. My heart sank; the wound was catastrophic. I was astonished he had survived at all, much less for the four days these three had been in hiding, waiting to flag down an unsuspecting ambulance driver.

His torso, hot to my touch, was peppered with oozing, blackened and crusty scabs — they were grisly enough, but the most savage trauma was confined to his lower abdomen.

Even the finest surgeons, in the most sterile operating theatre, in the world's best hospital would not be able to save him; the damage was just too great.

I registered the greenish-black hue of the surrounding, already bloating skin, and it was all I could do not to recoil at the foul, tell-tale odour of pus.

We had a system of classifying the wounded; trivial, treatable, and terrible. This man fell into, probably eclipsed, the last category.

I swallowed the lump lodged in my throat and faced his two friends.

"I cannot help him," I whispered. "He is already dead, but his spirit is not ready to relinquish his body."

I steeled myself for the backlash, the inevitable reaction to my failure. I sent up a prayer that someone would find my remains and tell my parents, then closed my eyes and pictured Thad, tall and handsome, his twinkling smile and intoxicating kisses.

"I am so sorry."

The pair frowned at me, uncomprehendingly. They had not understood.

"Ich kann ihm nicht helfen," I translated.

The soldier sitting alongside the dying man dropped his head into his hands and let loose a string of what I assumed to be curses, since I recognised the word *scheisse.*

His comrade simply muttered over and over again, "Nein. Nein. Nein…"

Their features crumpled, contorting in a grief that was palpable. I felt a sharp stab of sorrow for these lads who, by rights, ought to be studying at university, or helping their fathers on the farm, or some such benign occupation. Not killing strangers or skulking in a shed watching their friend die from horrific injuries.

"What is his name?" I asked in German.

"Lenz," my kidnapper replied.

"You two?"

"Anton, and he is Oskar." Anton gestured at the man seated next to Lenz.

I pointed to myself. "I am Polly, and now we know each other." Still using their language, I continued, "I can make him comfortable. Ease his pain." I essayed hopefully, my accent leaving a lot to be desired. The throbbing in my head had increased to epic proportions and I was struggling to focus.

"Bitte," Oskar beseeched.

I offered a tentative smile. "I shall do my best."

Fourteen

Polly

Delving once again into my satchel, I retrieved the tin in which were slotted phials of pain relief. Even though I knew their order, I still lifted it to the candle to ensure I chose the most potent — neither camphorated oil nor caffeine were going to cut it.

My fingers hovered over the morphine, not a drug I chose lightly, but better this than leave the poor boy to die in acute agony. I removed the vial and glass syringe, measuring the dose, although why that mattered, I do not know… training, it seemed was ingrained.

He did not flinch when I inserted the needle into his fragile vein, another indication of his pain levels but, gradually, the lines carved across his features relaxed, the tremors racking his body abated, and his breathing slowed.

Folding a piece of cloth, I mopped his face, pushing damp

strands of hair off his brow. "Sei friedlich, Lenz," I adjured quietly. *Be at peace.*

A curious hush descended on our bizarre tableau. Anton and Oskar stared at Lenz, their devastated expressions threatening to undo my resolve not to weep. Lenz was slipping away, passing over the threshold to whatever afterlife he believed in. Oddly, I hoped it was his version of heaven, not hell.

I lost all track of time, my concentration on Lenz and keeping him as comfortable as possible in the cramped little shed. The weather-beaten wooden structure had lost much of its integrity and offered little protection from the arctic draft.

By dint of another charade and undoubtedly lousy German, I asked Oskar to fill his helmet with snow. I rubbed some on my hands, then, as it melted, dipped the cloth in the cool water and moistened Lenz's poor cracked lips.

As the night marched on, uninterested in this — in the overall scheme of things — incidental battle between life and death, our fitful and largely disjointed conversations were marked by tiny puffs of air, ghostly in the weak candlelight.

No stranger to these final moments, I had not grown accustomed to them... and hoped I never would. Taking Lenz's hand, I stroked the icy cold skin and began to croon a Christmas carol.

Not any old Christmas carol, this one was composed by a German nearly a hundred years ago. The origins, haunting melody, and reverent lyrics seemed fitting.

"Stille Nacht, heilige Nacht..." I knew it by heart, all three verses, glad for Lenz when the other two joined in, our voices, ironically, in perfect harmony.

I watched for the signs indicating Lenz was leaving us and when they manifested, nodded to his friends. I sang on as, eyes suspiciously damp, they farewelled their comrade in their own way.

The rise and fall of Lenz's chest, stalled, and stopped for long seconds then, exhaling on a rasping rattle, he died.

Overwhelmed with sadness, I bent my head, pretending not to hear the ragged sobs from Oskar and Anton.

Giving them time to regain their composure, I smoothed gentle fingers over Lenz's eyelids, closing them forever, and covered him with one of the coats. Regardless of him being an enemy soldier, his body could not be left; they would fester and attract vermin. I could not countenance such desecration.

It might not be my call.

Without thinking, I opened the door to let the fresh air waft through and leant against the rickety jamb.

All around me, cloaked in darkness, the world was still. Even the snow had stopped, although I spied a few flakes gliding down from the night sky in leisurely pirouettes. It was at once both a winter wonderland and a frosted cage.

"Danke." A gruff voice spoke from behind me.

I turned and smiled wearily. "He is out of pain," was the best I could come up with. Trite, I know, but what else could I say? "You must rest." I mimed being asleep. "Tomorrow, we go, hospital. Morgen kommst du mit mir."

They looked at me in consternation, and I tried to alleviate their fears, but I was too tired to translate complete sentences. "Keinen Schaden. No harm." I drew a cross on my chest with one finger, hoping they understood the gesture. "I promise."

A hurried exchange ensued, and Anton said, "Ja, ok, wir kommen."

I managed to form an exhausted smile of acknowledgement and, ignoring the bells clanging in my head in dire warning that they might shoot me in my sleep, sank onto the floor, curled up into my coat, and shut my eyes.

Advanced Dressing Station
Hours Earlier
Private Walters

Driving with more haste than care, I had to brake sharply to avoid missing the entrance to the farmhouse, earning a spluttered oath and a glare from Private Dixon when we juddered to a halt.

"Watch it, we need to get this one back intact," he groused.

Taking no notice, I hopped down from the cab and hurried into the Dressing Station. Dixon on my heels.

"Any news?" I asked, knowing the answer before anyone updated me. Polly was not in the room.

"Nothing yet. There's a couple of lads scouring the area, but the elements are against us until daylight." Doc Carmichael jerked his head towards the window, and the encroaching darkness.

"Do we know what happened?"

Jim Travers interjected, "I've seen the wreck. There's very little blood. The ambulance took a battering, but there's none of the usual damage associated with an exploding mortar. If I was to hazard a guess, I'd say concussion grenade."

"Not one of ours, surely?" Private Dixon quizzed, stamping his feet both to rid them of snow and warm up.

Jim shrugged. "Possible. Won't know unless there's any trace of the casing. We searched the area, came up empty."

"Bugger." Dixon grimaced.

"Nowt we can do about the lass right now, but we can

help these two. They can't be lying here all night." Bob's tone reminded us of the reason Polly had driven here in the first place.

Conceding the doctor's point, we transferred the stretchers into the ambulance. "You'll let us know?" I called to Jim as the engine grumbled to life.

"'Course." He grinned and thumped the bonnet. "Take care."

No one — not the staff at the dressing station, nor Dixon nor I had dared voice the obvious.

Polly knew where the farmhouse was yet, as far as any of us could tell, had not tried to make her way here.

Under the darkening sky, I guided the vehicle out of the gate and turned right. Doing my best to avoid the worst of the potholes, we trundled along the uneven road.

As we approached the junction leading to the aid post, I slowed to a crawl.

"What?" Dixon frowned his confusion.

"How's about we nip down there to tell Archie about Polly? He could get a message to Warrant Office Jenkins."

Private Dixon twisted to face me. "Are you bonkers? The Dragon'll have our hides, not to mention what old Burrows'll say." Referring to the irascible chief surgeon of the FA.

"It'll take less than five minutes. We are not breaking regulations. How'd you feel if your girl was missing, and no one told you. In the middle of a war zone?"

At the grand old age of nineteen, Dixon, who lacked imagination and thought courting was soppy, opened his mouth to argue.

Before he got a word out, I reminded him how many

times Polly had brought him hot tea and a bacon butty at the end of his shift, that she never complained about working extra hours, that she had even knitted the gloves he was wearing.

"Fine, but don't dawdle," he capitulated grudgingly.

I grinned my victory.

Despite the snow, the route to the aid post was reasonably unobstructed. Archie appeared, puzzled at the arrival of an ambulance when, for once, there were no wounded… not even a frostbite case.

"Bloody 'ell." He whistled when I clarified our presence. "Right you are, Sid. I'll get a message to old Jenkins if I have to tek it meself."

"Much obliged." I raised a hand in acknowledgement, turned the ambulance, and headed back to the main road.

Within twenty minutes the two patients were under the care of one of the medical teams, and Dixon and I were inhaling piping hot stew.

Fifteen

Trenches - Front line, Foncquevillers
Thad

Uncomprehending, I stared at Archie, watching his mouth moving as he repeated the message. All I heard was garbled nonsense but made a concerted effort to decipher his words.

"Forgive me, Archie." Formalities had gone out of the window. "You need to run that by me again. Polly was in an accident and is now missing?"

"Sir." Archie nodded and explained Private Watkins' detour. "They are confident she is not badly hurt and 'ope she's found some shelter."

The shock struck me like a physical blow. Polly missing was bad enough, made ten times worse because I could not help search for her. *How can they be confident she is unharmed when they can't find her? There's a reason she has vanished off the face of the earth.*

By sheer force of will, I staunched the raft of troubling scenarios churning around my brain and expressed my gratitude to Archie. His job was not to act as an intermediary between military personnel.

"Thank you, Archie. I suspect Private Watkins bent a few rules to get that intel to you. If you see him before I do, please tell him, I appreciate it."

Archie grinned. "That I shall. Try not to worry, Warrant Officer. Polly's a smart lady and brave too. She'll be back afore you know it."

"I pray you are right. Watch yourself getting back, Fritz is playing dodge the bullet tonight," I cautioned, as, to underscore my point, the sky lit up in a volley of gunfire.

"Bloody Hun," Archie griped and, ducking his head, vanished from view along the snowy trench network.

I stood motionless, images of Polly chasing through my head. Fleeting moments, but no less treasured. In truth, we had scarcely met, and our courtship was only in its infancy. Her shifts and my infrequent rotations meant we had spent more time apart than together.

Our affection was not some passing phase sparked by circumstance, yet neither of us had articulated the depth of our devotion. Perhaps in fear of it being crushed before ever it had chance to soar.

Now, faced with the very real possibility, Polly was in danger, or lying hurt… incapacitated on land, which was hostile in more ways than one, I cursed myself for not telling her how much I loved her, that she was the other half of my soul, and that I wanted to spend the rest of my life with her.

"What's up?" Charlie Townsend appeared at my shoulder, jerking me from my regret-ridden reverie.

I dragged my mind back to reality, and reiterated Archie's message.

"Dammit it all to hell," Charlie scowled. "Sometimes I hate this war."

"*Some*times?" Against expectations I felt a twitch of amusement.

Charlie chuckled. "Well played. So, what're we going to do?"

"Do? We can't *do* anything. We're stuck here in someone's idea of a sick joke until we cop it, get sent home, or the fools who started it see sense." I heard my aggravation and pressed my lips together.

Charlie gawked. Not surprising, given this was the first time I had voiced my opinion publicly. Until this moment, despite the vicissitudes, setbacks, and struggles of the wretched war, I had held my tongue. Morale was already hanging by a thread; I did not want to be the one to wield the scissors.

"Sorry, Charlie, keep that to yourself. We don't need a mutiny on our hands."

"Sir." Straight faced, he added, "Last thing we need, is to break in another WO."

I could not help the grin, feeling my frustration ease, if only marginally. Charlie had stepped into Fred's shoes; his jovial optimism in the face of adversity, a boost to flagging spirits, and, I for one, was abidingly grateful.

"Who's due to rotate out?" he asked.

I reeled off a handful of names.

"So, let's ask 'em if they can spare an hour on their way back to camp. Not like there's anything spoiling."

"Not a bad idea at all, Corporal Townsend." I slapped him on the back. "Knew there was a reason we kept you."

My dread had not subsided but, at least, having a plan of sorts was reassuring.

. . .

I did not sleep a wink that night.

Shed — Middle of Nowhere
Polly

Aching muscles screamed their objection when I woke, momentarily baffled by my discomfort.

Memory flooded in.

I stayed where I was, waiting for my eyes to adjust, becoming aware that, although the inside of the shed remained dark, the merest lessening of the inky obscurity was discernible through the multitude of cracks in the rickety walls.

Wincing, I stretched, and yawned, amazed I had slept at all.

Narrowing my gaze, I scanned the miserable interior. I half-expected to be alone save a dead body; that Anton and Oskar had scarpered back to their regiment under cover of night.

A notion dispelled when I spied two awkward-looking shapes, hunched on the floor in front of me. I exhaled a silent sigh of relief.

I have no idea why I cared what happened to these two men. They, well Anton, had not given my sensibilities a single thought when he all but blew me up and kidnapped me, except I did not want them to die.

They might see out the war in a POW camp but, at least, they would see out the war. Get the chance to live long and happy lives, get married, have children, be productive members of society.

If they returned to their unit, they could be dead in a ditch tomorrow.

No, my way was better. All I had to do, was figure out how to get them back to the dressing station without us all getting shot.

I had every faith in my persuasive abilities.

Quietly, I tiptoed to the door and unlatched it. Sometime during the night, the snow had stopped, the heavy mantle of clouds yielding to a crisp, clear sky and a hard frost.

Above me, stars still twinkling, indigo was fading to the pearlescent silver of a winter's dawn.

Far to the east, the sun breached the horizon, ribbons of shimmering light bleeding through the trees and turning the monochromatic landscape into an artist's dream.

Rays of soft gold, trimmed with hues reminiscent of peony and carnation reclaimed the earth from the shadows.

The perfection of that morning stole my breath and remained etched in my mind forever.

Hearing movement behind me, I turned away from the beauty of nature to the far less picturesque scene in the shed.

"Guten Morgen," I greeted the two men who looked decidedly the worse for wear, prompting me to glance down at my own rumpled appearance. Who was I to talk?

A mumbled reply reached me, and I stifled a grin. "We must go. To the hospital," I said in German. "They will have hot food. We need to tell them about Lenz."

Trepidation slid over their grubby features like a mask, and I sympathised with their plight. Anton had abducted me… his laudable reasons notwithstanding… never mind the ruined vehicle. I had no idea whether it was salvageable and, if not, would be a costly loss.

Although Oskar was not directly culpable, neither of them could deny they deliberately targeted the ambulance with some kind of weapon, even if only one of them carried out the attack.

That I might have to argue their case gave me pause.

Would anyone listen to me? After all, I was nothing, a voluntary nurse and driver, ranked below that of the cooks in the canteen kitchen.

My evidence could tilt the scales against them, but I had faith in the integrity of the British military establishment and the tenets of the Geneva Convention. God willing, my trust was not misplaced.

Although my two Germans — yes, I had assumed a proprietary responsibility for them — were not wounded physically, other than cuts and scrapes, I would stake my life on them being maimed mentally; a cerebral trauma.

There were several schools of thought about this, ostensibly recent, condition, ranging from acute shock to cowardice.

As yet there was no definitive diagnosis, but cases were increasing.

We nurses had formed our own conclusions — the main one being that we doubted any 'condition' caused by conflict was recent — but kept them to ourselves and did what we could to treat those afflicted without drawing prejudicial attention to their plight.

There was a way of convincing whichever allied personnel we met first, that Oskar and Anton had surrendered to me but, whether the two in question would agree was a whole other matter.

In a peculiar mix of German, English, and theatrical gesticulations, I outlined my plan.

Fatigue must have addled their brains because neither man demurred.

My stomach rumbled, reminding me that I had not eaten for nearly twenty-four hours.

Time to face the music.

Sixteen

Polly

We plodded up the long drive to the farmhouse, easily located now, in the morning sunshine. I heard the slam of a door and saw two figures hurtling towards us.

I stepped out from behind the Germans, the rifle I was holding, a clear indication I was in control.

"Polly?" Bob Carmichael reached us first. His face reflecting his consternation.

"Morning, Doc. I found a couple of stragglers. Their English is…" I wobbled my hand, "…sketchy, but they could do with a cuppa and a bit of toast, if such a thing is available."

The doctor's jaw dropped at my breezy tone. "I… errr…" Nonplussed, he scratched his head.

"It's a long story. We are tired and hungry. This gun is really heavy. How on earth do our boys handle these things? Oh, and there's a body in yon shed." I managed a laconic smile.

"A body?" Sliding to a halt next to us, Jim Travers overheard this last.

"Yes, he shouldn't be left for the rats."

"German too?" Bob interjected.

"Yes but try not to hold that against him."

Jim opened his mouth, but I forestalled the predictable rebuttal.

"They're just kids. Jim. Yes, while their method of asking for help was questionable, they were desperate for someone to save their friend. Sadly, an impossibility. Surely, we can hand them over as POWs. Shooting unarmed men, enemy soldiers or not, is unacceptable."

I swayed on my feet, the rifle dipping to the ground as my grip slackened. "Please," I entreated.

Muttering under his breath about bleeding hearts, Bob took the rifle and guided the two Germans into the farmhouse, leaving Jim to loop an arm around my shoulders and all but carry me into the blessed warmth.

Within an hour, I felt restored. My head, the throbbing tapering off to a dull ache, had been checked, cleancd, and patched up. My hunger had been assuaged. I had enjoyed at least two mugs of tea... one, liberally laced with Brandy, which did not help my coherence one jot ... and had been able to freshen up — after a fashion.

My return was relayed to the FA, who dispatched Sid Watkins to fetch all four of us. Taking a stretcher, a couple of orderlies went to check the shed, conveying Lenz's body, which they had wrapped in canvas cloth, to the dressing station.

Jim explained what they thought had flipped the ambulance, and that they believed it was repairable, which came as a relief. One less mark against Anton and Oskar, whom —

we discovered much, *much* later — had no idea how much damage a concussion grenade could do.

It emerged, after a lengthy interview, that neither soldier had seen one in action… so to speak… before and expected nothing more than a shower of sparks. A diversion not a disruption.

By the time this information filtered down to me, all I could do was shake my head in dismay that those poor boys had been oblivious to the destructive nature of the weapons entrusted to them.

Sid's face was a picture. He all but ran into the farmhouse and, to my astonishment, engulfed me in bear hug.

"Thought we'd lost yer," he grumbled. "Took long enough to get you up to scratch. Can't face training another bloody driver."

"Take more than a concussion grenade to kill me," I sallied with a wink.

We bantered back and forth for a couple of minutes, while preparing to leave. I knew, once we reached the FA, the military police would assume jurisdiction for Anton and Oskar, possibly even Lenz… but I was rather vague about the protocols relating to dead enemy soldiers.

Nervous as to their fate, I was determined… all remaining equal… to put in my tuppenny worth before they were taken away. Evidently, my brush with death had induced an over-inflated sense of my own clout.

Safely stowed in the ambulance, we began the journey home. A word I never expected to associate with the drab assortment of tents, and the motley crew inhabiting them… but it had become, albeit temporarily, home.

The war may have forced us together, but our shared experiences had made us a family, however briefly, and I missed them. I even missed the Dragon, not that I would ever reveal that little nugget.

Expecting Sid to put his foot down and get us back as though Hades' hounds were after us — his customary driving style — I was surprised when he turned left down the winding track which led to the aid post.

"Sid?" I quizzed, raising a brow. "More wounded?"

"Not that I know of and, if anyone asks, we took a circuitous route because of snow drifts."

Parking, Sid climbed down and stuck his head around the partially collapsed segment of wall which served as Archie's centre of operations.

I heard a muffled conversation but was too far away to grasp the gist.

Archie appeared, along with a younger soldier who darted off into the trench network.

A flicker of hope ignited.

Surely not...

Trenches - Front line Foncquevillers
Thad

"Warrant Officer Jenkins. Warrant Officer Jenkins."

I glanced up at the sound of my name and stuck my head around the rime coated frame of what everyone euphemistically referred to as my office.

A soldier whose face was vaguely familiar came barrelling towards me. How he did not trip over the long legs of my men currently lounging at all angles against the walls of the trenches, doing everything in their power to stay warm was an impressive feat of nimble footedness.

"Keep low," I called a reminder. While the fusillades of gunfire had been intermittent of late, it did not pay to be complacent.

He grinned and stooped. "Warrant Officer Jenkins, Archie has asked you to come to the aid post sharpish like… oh, if you would be so kind," red-faced, he amended hastily,

I chuckled. "Don't fret…" I raised a brow in expectation of the lad's name.

"Private Shawcross," the lad introduced himself.

"…Private Shawcross. Right, let's see what's so urgent."

Asking Charlie to keep an eye on things and hoping all hell did not break loose in my absence, I followed Shawcross through the sinuous stretches of hollowed out channels to the rear of the network.

I was heading for Archie's improvised HQ, when my steps were arrested.

I blinked, not quite trusting my senses. *Was I imagining things? Was this an illusion wrought by desperation and desire?*

Next to an ambulance, a mite dishevelled, slightly pale, and sporting a bandage around her head, yet breathtakingly beautiful, stood the woman who had captured my heart.

"*Polly?*"

She smiled, and I swore the world stopped spinning.

"Polly." She was in my arms before she could utter a single word.

"Thad," blushing, she chided gently when we came up for air. "We have company."

"I could not care less if the entire allied armies are watching," I replied and, to prove my point, kissed her again.

An awkward cough shattered the idyll. I lifted my head but did not relax my hold. Aware Polly and Sid could not tarry, I had to know. "Do you have time to tell me?"

"I got blown up and kidnapped by a German soldier who wanted me to save his badly injured comrade. Couldn't and expected them to shoot me for failing. They did not and, in exchange, I persuaded them to hand themselves over," she recited the events of the previous night with studied nonchalance, but I spotted the set of her jaw and the sadness in her eyes.

"We must not dawdle," she murmured. "Sid just wanted…"

"I know." I pressed a kiss to the top of her head. "I'm not due a break for another few days, but I'll call in at the FA on my way to the encampment. You take care and don't bottle things up."

I leant back to rake what was becoming an experienced eye across her taut features. "Promise?"

"Promise."

Sid revved the engine.

"I have to go."

I cupped her face between my gloved hands.

It was not the time or the place, but I had to say it.

"I love you, Polly Armstrong."

She stared at me, a radiant beam quickly supplanting her stupefaction at my announcement.

"I love you too, Warrant Office Thaddeus Jenkins."

One more tight hug and she was gone.

Seventeen

Field Ambulance
Polly

I recall I had to endure a raft of formalities. All manner of reports, relating to every aspect of the incident had to be written and submitted.

I was examined by Mr Burrows who tutted and tsked, then pronounced me fit as a fiddle, but prescribed two days' rest on account of my sore head and impaired hearing.

There was definitely the luxury of a bath and a hair wash in there somewhere and, I'm pretty sure, the girls spoon fed me a huge portion of cook's amazing stew and dumplings.

Had my life depended on it, I could not tell anyone in which order these things occurred, because I was floating on a cloud of euphoria.

Thad loved me.

I thought the perception of sentiment was sufficient.

Apparently not.

The words reverberated around my head at random intervals, eliciting ripples of unadulterated delight and warming me all the way to my toes. *Who needed a stove?* I could not stop smiling, to the mock annoyance of the entire FA.

"Lordy, I hope he marries you and quick," Marjorie teased after asking me to pass the salt three times."

"Sorry, I was miles away," I apologised.

"Hmmm… about two miles to be exact," Cilla interjected slyly.

"Oh, hardy ha ha ha," I countered and feigned a scowl a gargoyle would struggle to better.

"My, my, what rapier wit." Cilla chortled, grabbing her stomach as though stabbed. "Is that the best you can come up with. Honestly, Armstrong, I despair."

I took their ribbing in good part. Quite frankly, cocooned in my little bubble of happiness, it rolled off me like water off a duck's back.

Five Days Later

True to his word, Thad sought me out on his way back to camp, tracking me down to the laundry tent where he found me elbow deep in dirty sheets.

The war seemed to be slumbering at the moment, so we had seized the advantage, and begun an exhaustive spring clean… knowing full well, that by spring, we might not even be here or, and more probably, be too inundated with casualties, to spare the time required to 'bottom the camp' as Staff called it.

Risking the Dragon's wrath, he came up behind me, slid his hands around my waist and brushed his lips to my nape.

"Polly." His breath, more a sensual sigh, skimmed my throat.

Utterly enchanting.

Goosebumps peppered my skin… nothing to do with the wintry conditions. Shaking off the soapy suds as best I could, I spun in his embrace, hooked my arms around his neck, and reciprocated, with unfettered fervour.

The tent, the camp, even the war faded into insignificance, as our pent-up ardour manifested in a kiss which went on and on until the very air seethed with the intensity of our emotions.

Prudence reared her decidedly unwanted head, and sanity triumphed over impetuous passion.

"Marry me?" Thad's question ought to have startled me, but it was as though I knew it was coming. That this moment was pre-ordained, eons before circumstance threw us together.

With Thad, I was home, safe and protected, loved and adored, honoured and respected. Never mind that his sinfully delectable kisses had the power to reduce me to a quivering wreck.

My fingers tiptoed down his serge jacket, a mischievous imp goading me to revel in the moment, to stretch it out. It was my first proposal of marriage. I hoped it would be my last proposal of marriage; it was only fair.

"Hmmm… marry you, you ask? That is a serious proposal. Pray tell, what does a tall, dark-eyed, dashingly handsome warrant officer have to offer a lowly VAD?" I said, instilling a languid note into my reply.

He smothered a snort of mirth. "Lowly? You? Nothing low— wait you think I'm handsome?"

"Dashingly so, and tall…" I reminded pertly, "…with dark eyes."

"The world, if I could but, and I concede it is a poor

substitute, my undying love forever." He bowed and pressed a kiss to the back of my hand.

Be still my beating heart.

"Oh well, in that case…" I grinned and bobbed a curtsy. "How could I possibly refuse."

"Is that a yes?"

I could see Thad was getting confused by our old-fashioned repartee.

"Of course, it is a yes, you darling man!"

Our betrothal sealed with another sizzling kiss.

I supposed our engagement would be protracted, that our wedding would be postponed until the war ended.

I underestimated Thad.

He refused to delay our nuptials, even knowing we could not live together as a married couple, our duty being to the army, not each other. Weddings were not encouraged among military personnel, especially so close to the front line but, where there is a will there is a way, and Thad was resolute.

Protocols, regulations, and mountains of paperwork ensued; the process was interminable — never had the phrase *the mills of the gods grind slowly* been more applicable. Just when I was beginning to think it was all too hard, we received the longed-for permission.

We asked the chaplain, a man we knew well, whether he had any objection to conducting the ceremony on New Year's Eve.

"I cannot think of a more felicitous date for the occasion." He smiled his agreement.

At which point, the FA went into overdrive.

1916 — New Year's Eve
Field Ambulance
Polly

Side by side, we stood in front of the chaplain. In place of traditional wedding finery, we wore our regular uniforms... which, at least, looked spick and span.

To my gratitude and astonishment, my friends had fashioned a bouquet with sprigs of winter foliage, tied with a bow made from a strip of bandage... the absolute height of extravagance.

The canteen which doubled as a chapel was adorned with greenery, and some clever person or persons had created several swags from sheets then draped them strategically around the old barn.

Outside, snow blanketed the ground, muffling all sound, and the atmosphere within was wonderfully festive.

I felt Thad take my hand and squeeze my fingers.

I turned and our eyes met.

I stared into his dark brown, twinkling gaze, and there, between heartbeats was my happily ever after.

Thad

I waited at the end of the makeshift aisle, generously decorated by Polly's friends. I confess, I felt more nervous today than when I married Sylvia. Sylvia — her delicate features drifted into my mind... *really Thad, how tactless, thinking of your first wife while preparing to plight your troth to your new bride.*

Curiously, and even while acknowledging how ludicrous it would sound to anyone else... expect, perhaps, Polly, I was consumed by the impossible impression, Sylvia was giving us her blessing, wishing us a lifetime of happiness.

Flight of fancy or not, I dipped my head in acceptance and, in the same gesture, let her go — consigning Sylvia to the past, as my future walked towards me.

Looking like an advertisement for a VAD recruitment drive, her silky hair twisted into an intricate style, I would relish unravelling later, Polly came to stand at my side. She nudged me with her elbow. I glanced at her, and she canted her head to grin at me, her glorious blue eyes sparkling. My nerves melted away.

I took her hand and interlaced our fingers.

The chaplain began the age-old liturgy, the reverent words resonating through me.

As he pronounced us man and wife, we faced each other.

Our eyes met, and my heart stuttered.

In that moment, in the middle of a war, I had found my sanctuary.

Eighteen

Ten years. I stared at the narrow gold band on my finger, recalling our wedding day.

The date had seemed… serendipitous — closing the door on the old and welcoming in the new.

No chance of a honeymoon to far-flung lands where peace reigned, but we were granted two days. Although not nearly enough time to say everything we needed to say, at least we could begin.

The war machine did not pause while lovers murmured endearments in the darkness, while inquisitive fingers and lips explored, beguiled, and seduced; while hearts thrummed a frantic rhythm, knowing this bliss was ephemeral.

That tomorrow was not guaranteed.

In the blink of an eye, we were thrust back to reality, to chaotic routines choreographed by ever-shifting battle lines. The FA moved, the Lincolnshires moved and, occasionally, our paths crossed; tiny beacons of light keeping us sane through the unremitting nightmare.

Four years into the horrific debacle, as the sultry heat of summer softened to the misty mellowness of autumn, rumours filtered through that the Germans were preparing to surrender.

We took no notice. We had heard it all before and discounted the claims as scuttlebutt.

They persisted.

By late October, it seemed inevitable but, not until it was confirmed by our Lieutenant-Colonel did we allow the seeds of hope to germinate.

On November 11th, the entire FA stood in the centre of the camp, waiting, still not quite believing.

At eleven o'clock the distant thump of the guns stopped.

No one spoke. Every single one of us savouring what was at once the eeriest yet most wonderful silence.

Then it was back to business as usual. We could not simply down tools and go home, there was a ward full of patients requiring our attention. Nevertheless, the knowledge these would be our last batch of wounded boosted our spirits.

As the year turned, we were demobbed. A slow process, given there was no real precedent, but eventually we were homeward bound. It was bittersweet, saying goodbye to people who had become closer than family. Assurances to keep in touch were made, even knowing it was unlikely.

. . .

Nettleby was even more beautiful than my recall.

Adjusting to civilian life was not as easy as I had anticipated. For a time, the lack of a strictly regulated regime left me antsy and out of sorts. As a married woman, I was expected to relinquish my responsibilities as an integral member of a busy medical team and assume the role of housewife.

I wanted to be both.

Our local doctor saved the day. Cognisant of my occupation, he asked whether I would mind helping him out in the surgery a couple of days a week. The perfect compromise.

By dint of pestering the authorities, I discovered Anton and Oscar had survived. Initially interned in France, later they were transported to England and saw out the war in Shropshire.

So settled did they become that both decided against returning to their homeland, married local girls and, using the trades taught while POWs, set up a carpentry business together.

I felt a tinge of pride that my pig-headedness might have contributed even in so small a way to their success.

Life moved on — it's sedate pace a balm.

Now, eight years later, we were back.

When Thad suggested we celebrate our tenth anniversary

in the place we pledged our lives to each other, I balked. Why revisit what was, essentially, a mass grave? A place steeped in terror and death.

I am endlessly glad I agreed.

The ravages of war had left an indelible scar, but the resilience of the human spirit could be seen everywhere.

We located the site of the FA, no longer recognisable except in our minds. Feeling like naughty children, we snuck through the gate and crossed the snowy field to where we gauged the canteen once stood.

In the winter tranquillity, at odds with our memory, we renewed our vows. The only witnesses a few hardy birds.

We had come full circle.

Thad

I knew suggesting we return to Foncquevillers might sound tactless but, as our tenth anniversary approached, the yearning to revisit the place where we swore to love and to cherish each other had become irresistible.

Polly's reaction was not unexpected. Then, just as I questioned whether I was the worst husband in human history, I noticed a myriad of emotions chase across her face and her consternation softened to perception.

"You want to lay the ghosts?" she quizzed.

"In part, but, in the main, I want to renew our vows where my soul first recognised its mate."

Her jaw dropped and a delicate shade of pink washed up her cheeks. "Thad... you old romantic."

I grinned diffidently. "Less of the old."

She gripped my hand and stretched up to kiss me... our ardour quickly spiralling out of control. Ten years, and she still had the power to bring me to my knees; a state of affairs to which I capitulated without a murmur of protest.

It was not dissimilar to the day we married; frosty air, and snow-blanketed ground, although this time there was no distant roar of gunfire, and the only witnesses were the birds.

In hushed tones, we recited the oath we first made a decade ago. A promise fulfilled every day, as much to honour each other as to honour the ones who never got the chance.

Wrapping Polly close, we stood together, recounting snippets of memory as they resurfaced.

I felt her shiver and brushed a kiss to her forehead.

"Time to go?"

She smiled, her blue eyes perhaps a little shadowed. "For now, but this place is part of us. I have a feeling we'll be back."

Thad

She was right.

Foncquevillers became our bolt hole, a quiet retreat away from the hustle and bustle, and not just for us. Several of our friends spent many a summer there, and loved it as much as we did.

A place which could so easily have haunted all of us, became a haven.

I cannot deny the war changed us. We went from blithe to cynical and, forced to face our mortality daily in the most heinous of ways, lost our innocence but, when hostilities ceased, we had a choice.

An armistice — defined as a formal agreement to end fighting. Not necessarily peace *per se*, but its precursor. A respite to take a step back and let sanity prevail.

Much as it was tempting to bear a grudge against those who made our lives a living hell, we too had to sign an armistice of our own.

We could either stagnate, wallow in hatred and bitterness, let the canker fester… or… take a step back to formulate a way to accept and move on. To forgive, even though we could never forget. To trust in the innate goodness of our fellow man.

Otherwise, all those who died to save humanity, died in vain. We had to make every day count… for them.

I'm only speaking for a small group of friends from an unassuming corner of Lincolnshire, but I reckon we did them proud.

Nineteen

11:00am — 3rd September 1939
Nettleby Under Wold
Polly

Six friends were huddled around the wireless set in our parlour. The soft, underlying hiss was not enough to obscure the words which battered us like hammer blows.

"This morning, the British ambassador in Berlin handed the German government a final note stating that unless we heard from them by eleven o'clock, that they were prepared at once to withdraw their troops from Poland, a state of war would exist between us.

"I have to tell you now that no such undertaking has been received and that, consequently, this country is at war with Germany," Mr Chamberlain's measured tones more compelling than the shouting and ranting of Hitler's rallies.

. . .

There was more, something about trying his best to avoid this outcome, but that Herr Hitler was determined to attack Poland regardless.

Unbidden, I ruminated over whether anyone else had registered the scheduling of this proclamation — 11am; the same time the armistice was declared twenty-one years ago.

Calculated or coincidental?

Watching the horror of the unfolding crisis darken the faces of our friends, I sent up a prayer of thankfulness that we did not have children.

While not a conscious choice either way, although something we had discussed at length, it transpired, after all we had witnessed, neither of us wanted to bring a child into a world where peace — despite earnest declarations that we had fought the war to end all wars — teetered on a knife edge.

We never regretted our decision.

I was, however, known for rescuing every animal in a ten-mile radius — good job I have an understanding husband.

Mr Chamberlain's voice pierced my musings, and I tried to focus.

"We have a clear conscience. We have done all that any country could do to establish peace. But the situation in which no word given by Germany's ruler could be trusted, and no people or country could feel itself safe, had become intolerable. And now that we have resolved to finish it, I know that you will all play your part with calmness and courage."

· · ·

I closed my eyes, feeling Thad's strong hand slide under mine and grip it firmly. This storm would be harder to weather. Our adopted nieces and nephews would be dragged into the conflict, the weapons were infinitely more destructive, and the notion my friends might lose their adored children rent my soul.

Biting my lip, I summoned up a smile and offered the national panacea. "Tea anyone?"

Later, as we prepared for bed, I gave vent to my feelings, "All those men who died so this would never happen again. They must be rolling in their graves." Scenes from those years rearing up in my mind.

"We had faith…" Thad did not need to finish his reply.

I shook my head and sank onto the edge of the bed. "I could weep."

He drew me close. "You won't be the only one."

Epilogue

31st December 1966
Nettleby Under Wold
Thad

Fifty years! Where did they go? I paused in the middle of my shave to study my reflection in the mirror... something I generally avoided, preferring not to linger any longer than necessary looking at my aging features.

Oddly, there remained an echo of youthfulness in the relatively smooth skin of my face, and my eyes, although requiring spectacles, still bore a twinkle of roguish charm — I liked to think so anyway.

Usually, we spent our anniversary in Foncquevillers and, it had become a treasured ritual, every ten years, to renew our vows in the same field... now with the amused permission of the owner.

The tranquil hamlet remained unchanged and unspoilt by the passage of time and tourism. Still just a tiny farming community where, I think, there were more graves in the military cemetery than actual residents.

This year, our friends wanted to celebrate with us, here in Nettleby. I am not a fan of large crowds and loud festivities… possibly a residue of that long-ago war… but once Lizzie, in her inimitable way, had convinced me it would be a modest gathering, I caved to the inevitable.

To be fair, a golden wedding anniversary is a major milestone. One, given where we said our vows, I never expected to toast. Memories of that day teased, and I smiled at the mirror — a miracle, for which I am eternally grateful.

I finished shaving, dried my face, and walked into the bedroom. Polly was sitting at the dressing table, staring at her reflection in much the same way as I had stared at mine.

I squeezed onto the seat next to her.

"Fifty years. Where did the time go?" I repeated my own thoughts.

Polly leant into me, and I breathed in her subtle fragrance, wishing I could tap into the virility of my younger self.

"I'm not so sure I'm a fan of this whole growing old lark," she murmured.

I slid my arm around her and kissed her temple. "At least we are fortunate to be growing old, love. So many did not."

She twisted to face me.

Our eyes met and the decades unravelled between us, like an autobiography in reverse.

Scenes from a lifetime of love, laughter, and boundless joy. Neither of us was perfect, we had our squabbles, everyone did, but we never let the sun set on a quarrel.

Early on in our marriage, I had discovered a far more satisfying way of settling a debate; a method I suspect Polly exploited shamelessly — not that I was complaining.

"Just think, if not for a war…" she grinned impishly.

"Ha. Even without that bloody mess, I'm sure, I would have found you and snatched you away from the bevy of suitors begging to court you."

She chuckled and swatted my chest. "Always the romantic."

"You'd better believe it, honey," I feigned an American drawl.

"I would rather stay here just the two of us, but we'd best get a move on. They'll be waiting for us."

Polly

"Just a moment…" Taking my hand, Thad drew me upright and moulded me against him. As one, we glided across the bedroom carpet in a slow dance whose melody was known only to us.

Delicious tingles began their familiar and tantalising glissade down my spine — I might be seventy-six, but I wasn't dead.

We swayed together, relishing the harmony.

"I love you, Thad Jenkins."

"I love you too, Polly Jenkins."

He bowed and brushed a kiss to the back of my hand.

Theatrically, I pretended to swoon.

He caught me to him, and we kissed — tenderly, languorously, our love a tangible thing, still smouldering after all these years.

We were among the lucky ones.

In between chaos and confusion, in between death and

destruction, in between heartbeats — we had found each other...

    ...and never let go.

Afterword

A Nettleby Postscript

By the time I came to the end of this story, a second trilogy was brewing at the back of my mind, set during WW2 and featuring the children of my original characters.

For a while it pestered, I even jotted down a couple of scenarios but, the more I pondered, the more I realised it was unnecessary, and might, in fact, dilute the impact of the WW1 series.

That said, after coming on this journey with me, I thought you might like to know what happened to Joe, Lizzie, and a handful of their friends and colleagues... especially those on the periphery of the stories... once they returned home.

As noted in *A Guardian Unexpected*, Joe and Lizzie had three children, Thomas, Rose, and Arthur.

Fred and Maisie, despite starting their family later than

most, were blessed with two daughters, Hope and Lilly, then twin sons, Guy and George.

As adults, all seven saw action in one form or another during WW2 but, by the grace of God, none were lost.

Thomas married Lilly, and they live in Wrawby with their two children. Thomas works with his father on the farm.

Rose married a Canadian naval officer, Donald, who swept her off her feet… literally… during Operation Dynamo — better known as the Dunkirk evacuation.

Arthur stayed in the airforce, following his dream of becoming a pilot. He was deployed all over the world… to his parent's well-concealed chagrin… before transferring to a civilian airline.

After the war, Hope was assigned to Berlin where she ran into Luke who three years her senior had, coincidentally, attended the same school as she. A whirlwind romance ensued and the pair wed within three months, which came as a shock to their friends and family, especially as Hope was always considered to be the sensible one. The couple remain utterly devoted to each other.

George and Guy married local girls. They took over the post office and, purchasing the adjacent premises, extended the little shop to accomodate the growing population of Nettleby. Maisie continued to help out when necessary.

Although Thad and Polly had no children of their own, they relished the role of uncle and aunt to their friends' offspring. The rest of their story, you have just read.

Charlie Townsend married a French girl, Amélie, who he met in a boulangerie of all places. They started their married life in France but, to everyone's surprise, decided to call Nettleby home. The villagers had softened a lot since

Maisie's arrival over a decade ago and, although initially sceptical of the newcomer... who they viewed rather like one might view an exotic bird... soon warmed to her unfeigned friendliness.

Like Thad and Polly, Charlie and Amélie were happy just the two of them. To be honest, they were so besotted with each other, there was no room for children.

Harry Alderton never married. He became a professor of art history at the Hull School of Art, immersing himself in a world of creation and beauty... the antithesis of what he had experienced during the war.

He was the first of the group to own a motor car, and was often seen flying along the roads in the manner of Toad in the avidly read Wind in the Willows. His hearing, badly affected by the explosion in 1916, did not recover completely, but he did not let that prevent him from attending every classical concert in a thirty mile radius.

Sid Watkins married Marjorie Elsey — who, they discovered, had grown up three streets away from Sid's family — and they had a veritable football team of children. A skilled mechanic... the result of his years fixing ambulances, Sid opened a garage, coaxing Marjorie to do the books in her spare time.

Cilla Brooke and Iris Graeme continued with their nursing careers, working their way up to become Matrons in their respective hospitals.

Cilla — determined she was not going to waste her training and give up her job for a man — was courted for years by an extremely patient Bob Carmichael who, by sheer fluke had taken a surgeon's position at the same establishment. Eventually, she capitulated to his gentle if unrelenting persuasion, and married him, claiming he wore her down. They are ridiculously happy.

Committed to her vocation, Iris never married, preferring to keep her suitors… of which she had many… at arm's length. Her chosen lifestyle was considered, by some, to be unorthodox… hedonistic even, but Iris cared not one jot. Surviving four years of war, with its accompanying privations and trauma, left her adamant that she would honour those who died by living her life to its fullest, exactly as she pleased.

Private Dixon sought his fortune in America. He made some bad investments and took a hit in the crash of '29 but, with inimitable style, picked himself up, dusted himself off and carried on. Won the jackpot at a casino, married a wealthy widow, and never looked back.

Jim Travers stayed in France. He had no family in England and after being demobbed, took a job at a local stables, subsequently buying his own stud and becoming a major player in the horse racing industry.

He too married a French girl, Noële. They live not far from Foncquevillers and, in their spare time, volunteer at Commonwealth War Grave sites.

The Dragon, otherwise known as Mrs Patricia Salisbury, continued with her vocation, and saw out her career as head of one of the new training schools. Widowed young, she never remarried, content in her own company. She *did* have a bevy of dogs who had her wrapped around their furry paws.

The second daughter of a viscount, Lady Rosamund Grey, better known to her subordinates as Staff, returned to her family's country estate in Norfolk, and got involved in a number of charitable causes.

Through one of these she met her husband, a very debonair earl, who fell in love with her on sight, and treated her like a queen…nothing more than she deserved.

Last but by no means least, Private Eric Burston… he of the maimed leg… was sent home from the front. Not one to sit on his laurels, as soon as he recovered, Eric began arranging care parcels for his fellow soldiers.

What began as small venture in his home town, evolved rapidly, and Burston's Boxes became a thriving enterprise, supplying home comforts to serving troops for the next fifty years.

Eric himself remained the same humble private, Polly had nursed in the summer of 1916, his anonymous philanthropy benefiting numerous humanitarian organisations.

I know the people, whose stories are entwined with that of Joe and Eliza — the couple who inspired this trilogy, my great grandparents — are fictitious, but their lives reflect the tenacity and resilience of those who refuse to let evil have its way.

The Nettleby Trilogy is my homage to them.

About the Author

Rosie Chapel lives in Perth, Australia with her hubby and three furkids. When not writing, she loves catching up with friends, burying herself in a book (or three), discovering the wonders of Western Australia, or — and the best — a quiet evening at home with her husband, enjoying a glass of wine and a movie.

Website: www.rosiechapel.com

Also by Rosie Chapel

<u>Historical Fiction</u>

The Hannah's Heirloom Sequence

The Pomegranate Tree - Book One

Echoes of Stone and Fire - Book Two

Embers of Destiny - Book Three

Etched in Starlight - Prequel

Hannah's Heirloom Trilogy - Compilation — e-book only

Prelude to Fate

Legacy of Flame and Ash

The Nettleby Trilogy (WW1 Novellas)

A Guardian Unexpected - Book One

Under the Clock - Book Two

Between Heartbeats - Book Three

<u>Regency Romances</u>

The Linen and Lace Series

Once Upon An Earl - Book One

To Unlock Her Heart - Book Two

Love on a Winter's Tide - Book Three

A Love Unquenchable - Book Four

A Hidden Rose — Book Five

The Daffodil Garden

The Unconventional Duchess

Rescuing Her Knight - *the de Wiltons:* Book One

Elusive Hearts - *An Unexpected Romance*: Book One

Shrouded Hearts - *An Unexpected Romance*: Book Two

His Fiery Hoyden

A Regency Christmas Double

Fate is Curious

A Christmas Prayer *with Ashlee Shades*

Luck be a Pirate

The Highwayman's Kiss

The Lady's Wager

Winning Emma

A Love Impossible

Unravelling Roana

Love Kindled

Moonbeams and Mistletoe

<u>Fairy Tale Romance</u>

Chasing Bluebells

<u>Contemporary Romances</u>

Of Ruins and Romance

All At Once It's You

Cobweb Dreams

Just One Step

His Heart's Second Sigh

<u>With Rori Bleu</u>

Evie's War

Vindicta

Corrupt Covenant

Lesser of Two Evils

Deadly Incision

The Hunters - Dystopian Fiction

Echoes & Illusions - Book One

Smoke and Mirrors - Book Two

The Sela Helsdatter Saga

A Flip of The Coin - Book One

Conceived Chaos - Book Two

Odin's Bane - Book Three

Valhalla's Doom - Book Four

Arcane Alchemy - Freya's Fate: A Helsdatter Saga Novella

Historical Fiction/Romance

The Pomegranate Tree

Hannah's Heirloom - Book One

Hoping to trace the origins of an ancient ruby clasp, a gift from her long dead grandmother, Hannah Wilson travels to the fortress of Masada with her best friend, Max.

Strange dreams concerning a rebel ambush begin to haunt Hannah and following a tragic accident, she slips into the world of Ancient Masada.

A woman out of time, Hannah must rely on her instincts and her knowledge of what will befall this citadel to survive.

Will she escape, or is she doomed to die along with hundreds of others as Masada falls — and what does any of this have to do with an ancient ruby clasp?

***

Echoes of Stone and Fire

Hannah's Heirloom - Book Two

Pompeii - a vibrant city lost in time following the AD79 eruption of Vesuvius. Now rediscovered, archaeologists yearn for an opportunity to uncover the town's past.

Some things, however, are best left alone - revealing the secrets hidden beneath the stones could prove perilous.

Hannah and Max are brought to Pompeii by a surprise invitation to join an excavation team who are trying to uncover the city's long history.

After entering an excavated house that bears a Hebrew inscription, Hannah's two worlds collide, and she falls back through time to ancient Pompeii. A place where her ancestor is a physician to gladiators engaged in mortal combat, where riotous mobs run amok and where a ghost from the past returns to haunt her.

Will Hannah and her loved ones manage to escape the devastation she knows is coming, before the town is engulfed in volcanic ash? Will she ever find her way back to Max the love of her life, waiting not so patiently millennia away?

Or will echoes be all that remain?

***

Embers of Destiny

Hannah's Heirloom - Book Three

AD80 - Hannah and Maxentius must embark on a new journey to Northern Britannia.

This harsh frontier is far from the comforts of Rome and danger lurks where least expected; a garrison of soldiers, some unhappy with their isolated posting; local tribes, outwardly accepting of their Roman occupier, but who may still resent the seizure of their lands.

Millennia away, Hannah Vallier finds a familiar item while working in a museum near Hadrian's Wall. It is the pomegranate; carved by Maxentius on Masada. Before Hannah can discuss it with Max, disaster strikes!

Believing her husband has been killed, Hannah retreats into the past, her soul melding with that of her ancestor, but with little idea of what they could face. Is the risk from the conquered tribes, or much closer to home?

As rebellion threatens to shatter a fragile peace, Hannah's heart whispers that just maybe Max isn't dead and that he is calling her home.

Can she trust her heart, or will she remain caught out of time, her destiny floating away like embers on a breeze?

***

Etched in Starlight

Hannah's Heirloom - Prequel

Maxentius - a Roman soldier fresh from the battlefields of Armenia, arrives to take command of the military outpost of Masada, Herod's isolated citadel in the Judaean desert.

A seemingly mundane posting after years of warfare, Maxentius finds it more challenging to maintain a focused garrison than to face the wrath of the Parthians across a disputed frontier.

Hannah - a young Hebrew physician spends her days dealing with injuries from street brawls, deprivation, disease and loss. As her beloved Jerusalem plunges into chaos, her brother — who belongs to a band of rebels determined to drive out their Roman occupiers — tells her of their plans to storm a desert fortress and steal the weapons stored there, persuading his reluctant sister to go with him.

Masada - following the ambush, Hannah finds and treats three badly wounded Roman soldiers. In the aftermath and against impossible odds, Hannah and Maxentius realise that they are more than healer and captive, their fate already etched in starlight.

Prelude to Fate

For Lucia, staring into the jaws of an horrific death, escape seems impossible.

Rufius Atellus, a veteran Roman soldier, is appalled when he recognises one of the victims about to be executed. Surely this is a ghastly mistake?

A ferocious she-wolf, anticipating a tasty meal, suddenly finds herself under a human's control.

In an unexpected twist, and as danger threatens, the lives of all three become inextricably entwined.

Was it chance brought them together in that theatre of bloodshed,
or simply a prelude to fate?

Legacy of Flame and Ash

A Hannah's Heirloom Story

An unremarkable family ring — lost when its owner was killed in
the catastrophic eruption of Vesuvius — is excavated after nearly
two millennia buried under tons of pumice and ash, setting off an
extraordinary sequence of events.

A brazen robbery, and the ring is lost again. The theft and
subsequent investigation, inspire twelve-year-old Cristiano Rossi to
dedicate his life to the search and recovery of stolen artefacts.

Fast forward twenty years. Whispers of a rare item being offered for
sale on the black market, initiates a joint operation between the
Italian and British branches of the, colloquially named, Art Squad.

Hannah Vallier and her tech savvy assistant, Bryony Emerson —
whose abilities to track down the untraceable, led to them assisting
the UK Art and Antiquities Unit — have unearthed an intriguing
thread.

Reluctantly, Cristiano agrees to team up with the pair to thwart the
traffickers, retrieve the artefact and, hopefully, dismantle the site.

What ought to be a routine assignment is complicated by a rogue
operative, an unexpected romance, an ancient connection, and a
very angry ghost!

The Nettleby Trilogy

A Guardian Unexpected

Book One

August 1914: Europe is on the brink of catastrophe. In a small village in rural Lincolnshire, a wife kisses her husband goodbye.

Childhood sweethearts, Eliza and Joe have only been married two years. They could not have imagined how soon they would be torn apart by war, nor that the most unexpected of guardians would offer them hope during their darkest hours.

***

Under the Clock

Book Two

England 1908: Under the clock, on a sleepy station platform nestled in rural Lincolnshire, an unexpected romance blossoms.

Maisie: Every Friday, at precisely five to six, a handsome young man arrives at the station. I know the time because I can see the clock. The train pulls in, punctual as always, and among the alighting passengers is an elderly gentleman. The young man greets him with a smile and a handshake, then tucks his arm through the older man's and they leave the platform.

Every Friday.

Occasionally, we exchange a glance or two and, to be fair, I suspect I notice him more than he notices me.

Fred: I count the hours until Friday afternoon comes around. Not only because this marks the start of the weekend but also, and more importantly, I get to see the flower girl. I am clueless as to her name, yet my heart begins to race the minute the station comes into view. I almost run up the steps onto the platform, hoping for a glimpse of her bright smile.

Every Friday.

I doubt she ever notices me. I'm just a village lad, one more faceless person in the throng.

Then again, you never know what might happen… in an innocuous corner of a quiet platform…

…under the clock

***

Between Heartbeats

Book Three

1916 — France

Polly

Nothing in my training, nor the numerous lectures I endured prior to leaving England prepared me for the horror that is trench warfare.

Assigned to a Field Ambulance — a sneeze away from the front line — the atrocities I witnessed were confronting, harrowing, and a constant challenge to my faith in humanity, yet the experience proved to be endlessly rewarding.

Not content with nursing, the principle reason I volunteered was to drive ambulances. My colleagues, preferring the relative safety of the wards, thought me addled, but I was not to be thwarted, despite the dangers. Saving lives outweighed the fear of being blown up or shot.

The last thing I expected to find in the midst of flying shrapnel was love.

Thad

Two long years with no end in sight; the oft repeated, 'we'll be home by Christmas' — a long-forgotten dream, supplanted by the ceaseless thunder of artillery, acres of mud, collapsing trenches, and the all-pervading stench of death.

A nightmare tempered when the driver of the ambulance dispatched to collect Fred, after his brush with a sniper, turned out to be Polly Armstrong, friend of Fred's wife, Maisie.

The initial shock of recognition morphs into something else; something both tantalising and terrifying.

Anyone with an ounce of common sense would quash such

frivolous nonsense; we were in the middle of a battle zone. Clearly, common sense had abandoned me.

Against the odds, in the chaos and confusion of war, romance blossoms but tomorrow is not guaranteed. In that split second between heartbeats, their happily ever after could be snatched away.

Regency Romance

Once Upon An Earl

Linen and Lace - Book One

When Fate saw fit to intervene in the life of Giles Trevallier, the very respectable Earl of Winchester, by dropping a female — soaked to the skin and with no memory of who she is or how she came to be there — literally at his feet, no one could have predicted the outcome.

While uncovering her identity, Giles realises he is falling hopelessly in love with his mystery guest, who unbeknownst to him, is succumbing to similar emotions; but, when the heart is involved, a thoughtless word or gesture can thwart even Fate's best-laid plans.

Faced with misunderstandings, whispers of scandal, secret documents and foreign agents, their chance at a happy ever after seems elusive, but fairy tales often happen when least expected, and love — however inconvenient — usually finds a way to conquer all.

***

To Unlock Her Heart

Linen and Lace - Book Two

Abused by a duke, and shunned by Society, relief seems at hand when Grace Aldeburgh is bequeathed a house in a small village, far from malicious gossips.

Once there, a tentative friendship blooms between Grace and Theo Elliott, the local doctor, who has already resolved to be the man to unlock her heart.

Just when happiness appears to be within her grasp, her erstwhile tormentor once again stalks Grace. After a failed kidnap attempt, the duke's quest culminates in an acrimonious confrontation, and the reason for his venal pursuit becomes agonisingly clear.

***

Love on a Winter's Tide

Linen and Lace - Book Three

Every day, Helena disappears into a world few acknowledge, helping the poor, downtrodden, and abused. A husband is the last thing she can be bothered with.

Busy managing his shipping line, Hugh Drummond sees no need for a wife, whose only joy is dancing and frivolity. If — and it was a huge if — he ever married, it would be to a woman as capable as he, not some giddy society Miss.

Then, Hugh meets Helena and despite their resolve, fate, it seems, has other ideas. As their attraction deepens however, treachery threatens to tear them apart. Will they uncover the perpetrator in time, or will their love be swept away, lost forever on a winter's tide?

***

A Love Unquenchable

Linen and Lace - Book Four

Jessica Drummond, a bright and cheerful young woman, rarely gives romance, let alone love, a thought. Long hours working in her brother's shipping office affords little chance of her ever meeting an eligible bachelor.

Duncan Barrington, veteran of the Napoleonic Wars, believes himself wounded in both body and soul. He has no intention of inflicting his demons on anyone, certainly not a beautiful and, in his opinion, irresponsible city lady.

One cold and snowy morning, the plight of a bedraggled puppy throws Jessica and Duncan together and, as a spark of something indefinable yet wholly unquenchable begins to burn, it is unclear who rescued whom.

***

A Hidden Rose

After witnessing his mother's grief at the loss of his father, Nick Drummond resolved never to cause someone he loved such distress. Even the happiness of his siblings would not sway him — until he met Rose.

Rose Archer was almost content assisting her doctor father in a tiny fishing village in the north of Yorkshire. To experience the world beyond, a tantalising dream — until she met Nick.

Unexpectedly, the impossible becomes possible, and the renounced — desired above all things, but the shipwreck that brought them together, may yet tear them apart. Will Nick learn to trust his heart, or will his love for Rose remain forever hidden

The Daffodil Garden

Horrifically scarred during the war, William Harcourt - Marquis of Blackthorne - prefers to spend his days in the quiet of his daffodil garden; plants do not pity, turn away, or judge.

Lucy Truscott, whose life is far removed from that of the *ton*, has no idea that by saving the life of a young woman, to whom she bears an uncanny resemblance, her own will be placed in mortal danger.

A chance encounter leads to something more. William begins to trust that Lucy sees the man beneath the scars, while Lucy is persuaded that love might actually transcend status.

Unfortunately, before their courtship has really begun, someone has every intention of ending it - permanently.

The Unconventional Duchess

Refusing to suffer the humiliation of her husband flaunting his mistress at Society events, the newly married Duchess of Wallingstead, Ella Lennox, takes control of her life. She leaves London for the family's country seat in remote Yorkshire.

A woman alone, Ella spends the next four years turning a cold, grim house into a home, and transforming the fortunes of the estate. Not afraid of hard work, she soon earns the respect of those around her with her determination and unconventional attitude.

Out of the blue, the duke arrives. Resigned to another arduous visit, Ella is stunned when it seems he is attempting to court her.

Impossible!

Could her dream of a happy marriage be about to come true?

Everything hangs on a snowstorm, a herd of cows and an uninvited guest!

Rescuing Her Knight

The *de Wiltons* — Book One

A story, invented to keep a little girl distracted, marks the beginning of another tale. One destined to remain unfinished for twenty years.

At thirteen, Adam Marchmain became Kitty de Wilton's 'Knight of the Garden' — a title bestowed following an accident which resulted in six-year-old Kitty having her knee sutured. Kitty never forgot his gallantry, but pledges made as children rarely survive into adulthood.

Their paths separated until Fate decreed, they meet again.

Widowed, badly disfigured and his sight ruined, Adam returns to his family home, a shadow of his former self.

Similarly afflicted, although her scars are invisible, Kitty — against her better judgement — is persuaded to help Adam banish his demons. This requires a subterfuge which, if discovered, might shatter more than the bonds of friendship forged two decades previously.

To Kitty, determined to break through the shield Adam has erected, the risk is worth it.

To see his smile and hear his laughter.

To rescue the knight of her childhood.

Just when a fairy tale ending is within her grasp, Kitty is threatened by the man who murdered her husband. In a cruel twist the tables are turned, and Kitty is the one who needs rescuing.

Elusive Hearts

An Unexpected Romance — Book One

What happens when two people whose elusive hearts fight an indefinable attraction, neither looked for nor desired, dare to dream?

When her fiancé and sister abscond to Gretna Green on her wedding day, Sapphira Beresford longs to escape, to avoid the gossipmongers gloating over her misfortune. Disillusioned, she is determined not to be burnt again, swearing off romance and marriage.

A fortuitous invitation sees her embarking on a journey to Pompeii where she meets Leofwin Colleville, reclusive marquis, amateur antiquarian, and her host for the duration.

Although enamoured of the ruins gradually being unearthed and ecstatic to have the opportunity to assist, Sapphira is troubled by her host's attitude, which blows hot and cold.

A confirmed bachelor, Leofwin Colleville is happiest surrounded by ancient ruins, and would prefer to brave the whole of Napoleon's armies alone, than face a lady on the hunt for a husband. The arrival of an unexpected guest throws his unencumbered existence into turmoil, but the harder he strives to maintain his distance, the more she gets under his skin.

Sparks fly and, as Leofwin's truculence undermines Sapphira's already battered confidence, her adventure of a lifetime seems doomed to disaster.

Until the day she runs afoul of greedy treasure hunters.

In the aftermath what was scorned becomes the one thing they crave above all else, but when it comes to the heart, nothing is ever simple.

***

Shrouded Hearts

An Unexpected Romance - Book Two

For the sin committed...

When the unexpected death of her much older husband, frees Madeline Galleron from a seemingly inescapable nightmare, she decides, as a way to regain her self-respect, that a little retribution is in order.

Working for Lucas Withers, Wolfstan Colleville, the Viscount Carnforth, finds himself assigned to a curious case of blackmail. One which involves, of all things, a dead rose, a poem and, at least, two victims.

Wolfstan's investigation leads him to an unlikely culprit and, as an entirely new plan is concocted, emotions believed forever vanquished are kindled.

A spirited woman, Madeline refuses to let her past dictate her future… *but…* to conquer her torment and take a chance on love, is a whole other matter. Dare she trust Wolfstan to be an honourable man with no ulterior motive? *Could* he be her knight in shining armour?

Can she open her heart, or will it remain forever shrouded?

His Fiery Hoyden

A Novella

Livvy has no respect for the nobility; they let her down when she most needed them. Why should she accede to their demands now?

Philip, Lord Harrington, is stunned to discover the young heir to the dukedom lives a stone's throw away in a ramshackle cottage, and resolves to restore the child to his birthright.

They meet in a clash of wills, but just when it seems Livvy might surrender, the victory Philip desires, may not taste all that sweet.

A Regency Duet

Luck be a Pirate

Luck wasn't something retired pirate Kennet Alexson believed in — good or bad. However, even he had to concede that landing a job at Trentams shipyard, and meeting Lynette Collins, was more than coincidence.

Fortune it seemed, was smiling on him for once.

As Kennet adjusts to life on dry land, his friendship with Lynette deepens into something far more enduring, and what once seemed elusive now becomes possible.

Unfortunately, fate has other plans, and Kennet's good luck is about to run out.

***

The Highwayman's Kiss

Surrendered Hearts — Book One

Nothing exciting had ever happened to Juliette St Clair.

Her days were spent assisting her father or calling on friends, wandering art galleries, taking constitutionals or, and more preferably, escaping into her books. Her evenings her evenings — an endless round of balls, where she preferred to remain invisible.

Until the day she was robbed by a highwayman.

A Regency Christmas Double

Heart Rescued

Four years since Jasper lost the woman he was hoping to marry. Four years since he closed his heart and withdrew from Society. He has no idea his reclusive existence is about to be shattered.

Enter his sister's best friend, Harriet, a flame haired beauty, who needs his help.

Reluctantly he agrees and as they spend time together, it is clear their feelings run deep. Although Harriet affects Jasper in a way no woman ever has, he believes her to be out of his league ~ but it's Christmas and she might just be the one to melt his frozen heart

***

Catch a Snowflake

Romance often blossoms in the most unlikely of places - but in a ward full of wounded soldiers - surely not?

When Lucas Withers comes face to face with Jemima Parsons - a young woman who blames him for her brother's injury - falling in love is the last thing on their minds. What neither of them anticipated, was the magic of snowflakes.

Fate is Curious

A Novella

Happily, ever after? No such thing! Bereft, following her beloved husband's sudden death, Lady Charlotte Sherbrooke has lost her belief in romantic nonsense.

Successful shipping merchant, Zacharie Romain, is no stranger to loss; his business can be hazardous. Moreover, his wife died in childbirth and even though it happened a decade ago, he has no mind to expose himself to such sorrow again.

They meet in less than joyful circumstances but, as the year turns and grief diminishes, the woes of a small boy become the catalyst for something wholly unexpected. Can Charlotte and Zacharie trust what Fate has in store or will past heartbreak prevent them from taking a chance on love?

A Christmas Prayer

with Ashlee Shades

A Short Story

An entreaty from a frightened child.

Orphaned and only nine, Caroline Thorne has to grow up before her time. She is doing everything she can to keep what is left of her family together and out of the workhouse but is terrified her prayers are not being heard. Or maybe they are…

A petition from a woman desperate for a family.

A chance meeting with three orphaned siblings, tugs at Elizabeth Barrington's heart strings. Thus far, she and her husband have not been blessed with children and, as Christmas approaches, a plan begins to form - one which might just be the answer to her prayers.

Two Christmas prayers, as different as they are the same.

Will they hear and, more importantly, heed the answer?

The Lady's Wager

Surrendered Hearts - Book Two

A Novelette

Ged Mowbray will do anything to avoid being married off to the suitable prospects his parents insist on parading in front of him.

Melissa Bouchard is under no illusion her sizeable dowry is the attraction to suitors, not her.

An overheard conversation leads to an offer too good to refuse, but what happens when a lady's wager, becomes a gamble on the happily ever after, you did not even realise you wanted?

Winning Emma

Surrendered Hearts - Book Three

A Novelette

Randolph Craythorpe — earl, covert operative, and occasional highwayman — believed his dalliance with Lady Felicity Hartwich would lead to marriage. It did, but not to him! The arrival of an unwelcome guest, however, provides the perfect opportunity to indulge in a little retaliation.

Emma Newbury accompanies her cousin, Lady Charity Anscombe, to London for the Christmas season. Once there, she comes face to face with the three men who witnessed the humiliating aftermath of her father's disgrace — one of whom, to her irritation, has taken up residence in her dreams.

Their infrequent encounters only serve to confuse but, while winter tightens its grip on the city, what was inconceivable becomes the one thing for which they both yearn, yet bound by Society's rules, cannot admit.

As the snow falls, Randolph begins to understand that to win Emma, he will have to surrender.

Moonbeams and Mistletoe

Surrendered Hearts - Book Four

A Novelette

If we are part of a universe where moonbeams and mistletoe exist, nothing is insurmountable for, otherwise, what is the point?

To Emily Livingston, spinster — this deceptively frivolous phrase was all she had left of her betrothed.

To Henry Bartholomew, widower — the sentiment, while naïve, also serves as a reminder that even in the darkest of hours, light can be found… it was simply a matter of perspective.

When four-year-old twins run into Emily — literally — she has no idea where their unexpected encounter will lead. Determined to ensure his children are *not* being schooled into something nefarious, Henry resolves to meet this mysterious lady who has enthralled the duo with her stories.

One dull and otherwise ordinary autumnal morning, two disparate souls are brought together, and long-forgotten emotions are stirred.

The question is whether Henry and Emily have the courage to follow their hearts or be forever trapped in the sadness of the past. Can moonbeams and mistletoe persuade them, the answer was there all along?

A Love Impossible

A Regency M/M Novelette

Tasked with investigating a heinous crime, Edward Lindsay travels from London to Dublin — a city which holds too many memories — in the guise of guardian to his sister. He knew it could be hazardous, and relished the challenge, but that wasn't what caused his stomach to tighten as they approached landfall.

Dublin held more than just a murderer.

There was also Aidan.

While attending a party, Aidan Griffen is astonished when he comes face to face with a man who fled Dublin two years previously. A man he has desperately tried to forget.

As Edward closes in on his quarry, a fire, deliberately extinguished, is rekindled. But what of it? Edward and Aidan share a love impossible, and to acknowledge their feelings — more dangerous than confronting a killer.

Is there any hope of a happily ever after?

Unravelling Roana

A Regency Novelette

Tired of being ignored by her husband, Roana Dumont, Countess of Brooketon does the one thing guaranteed to get his attention. She runs away… to Venice, leaving behind a set of riddles for him to solve… *if* he feels their marriage is worth saving.

Gideon Dumont, 6th Earl of Brooketon is flabbergasted when he discovers his wife has apparently vanished off the face of the earth. A series of puzzles, the only clue as to her whereabouts.

The question is… will he unravel them?

Love Kindled

A Regency Novelette

Recently widowed, Amelia Ingram - Countess of Gresham, decides to shake off the fetters from her arranged and loveless marriage.

Exploiting her new-found independence, Amelia indulges her yearning to explore - incognito.

Her ploy works so well, she receives an offer of employment from the dangerously handsome, Rupert Latimer - Earl of Badlesmere. On impulse, she accepts and finds herself governess to Cate, a delightful scamp of a child. What began as a bit of a game on Amelia's part, evolves into something far more profound, and a flame she presumed impossible to ignite, is kindled.

An unexpected turn of events leads to yet another offer. This time there is far more at stake and, determined history not repeat itself, Amelia confesses her ruse.

Rupert has been burnt once. Will he douse the spark, or take a risk and trust his heart?

Fairy Tale Romance

Chasing Bluebells

A Fairy Tale Novella

Once upon a time, somewhere in France, there was a man whose reckless obsession led him down a dark path — one which, ultimately, cost him his life.

That ought to have been the end of it.

Regrettably, as is so often the case, those who least deserve it, suffer for the actions of others.

A decade after being sent away, Sebastien Daviau returns to the little village where everything began. Hoping to lay the ghosts of his childhood to rest, he studiously ignores the possibility, he might run into Charlotte de Montbeliard.

As luck would have it, Charlotte is the one who runs into him… well, his horse… and although the brief encounter leaves a lasting impression, neither recognises the other.

A name revealed causes a freak accident, catapulting Sebastien's past into his present, and bringing him face to face with a man whose reputation would intimidate the most ardent of suitors.

Can whatever is blossoming between Charlotte and Sebastien survive the challenge imposed, or is their happily ever after about to fade as quickly as the bluebells they loved to chase?

Contemporary Romance

Of Ruins and Romance

Kassandra Winters has intrigued Gabriel St Germain since he accidentally knocked her flying outside her university professor's office. Her face haunts his dreams, yet he never expected to see her again. So, he is surprised when she appears, as though destined to do so, in the middle of a ruin, and he concocts a plan to win her heart.

Gabriel's old-fashioned courtship touches something deep inside Kassie and, although struggling to believe someone as handsome as Gabriel could possibly be interested in her, she soon realises she has fallen irrevocably in love with him. However, just as Kassie shares everything of herself with Gabriel, her world comes crashing down.

Can their romance survive, or will it fall in ruins, like the relics of antiquity that brought them together?

All At Once It's You

When Alex arrives in the small village of Rosedale Abbey, to take up a position as a research assistant for a renowned archaeologist, the last thing she is looking for, or expects to find, is love.

Jake was perfectly happy with the status quo. When it came to relationships, he didn't do committed or long term. He called the shots, and if his current flame didn't like it, she knew what to do. A philosophy, which served him well - until he met Alex.

Romance blooms, but even as the untamed wilderness of the North Yorkshire moors weaves its spell, a long-buried secret might yet jeopardise their happily ever after.

Cobweb Dreams

A Novella

A holiday on the Scottish isle of Mull was just the break Chloe Shepherd needed, an escape from her boring office job and her complete lack of anything resembling a social life. Romance, it seems, isn't on the cards and, although Chloe dreams of finding her soulmate she is beginning to believe love is like cobwebs — spun overnight, only to vanish in the early morning breeze.

Under sufferance, Dominic Winters makes a flying visit to Mull to check on a rental property owned by his family. He hasn't got time for this — so indulging in a holiday fling is the last thing on his mind.

A lamb stuck in a bog proves a most unexpected matchmaker and, while Mull weaves its magic, Chloe wonders whether those fragile cobwebs might be far more stubborn than she thought.

Just One Step

A Short Story

In the aftermath of an horrific car accident, Daisy Forrester travels to Italy - hoping, so far from her memories, she might begin to heal.

Archaeologist, and single father, Adam Willoughby is too busy looking after his young daughter to give romance let alone love, a thought.

Neither expects a chance encounter in an ancient ruin to be anything more, but sometimes, that's all it takes.

His Heart's Second Sigh

A Novella

Reuben Faulkner and Paige Latimer are two happily single people, who have no desire to upset the status quo.

Unexpectedly, they are thrown together, only to discover both want far more than a casual friendship.

Just when things take an interesting turn, Reuben's past catches up with them, and threatens to derail their blossoming romance before it has chance to start.

With Rori Bleu

Evie's War

World War II catapulted ordinary people into extraordinary service to save the world from an insidious evil... even if that meant being forced to do things which, under normal circumstances, would be considered abhorrent.

Genevieve Rousseau, Evie to a select few, was one such person who could not escape this fate. Despite her covert endeavours to liberate Paris from the Germans, she finds herself labelled a collaborator and an enemy of the French Republic.

Her only hope of vindication lies in helping a dangerously handsome American, with questionable motives, to uncover the Germans' final revenge.

Could struggling to resist Major Jack Donovon prove to be the decisive battle in Evie's War?

Vindicta

Nightmares come in many guises… but usually fade with the dawn…

Not so for Bobbi Jo Fletcher. A witness to the massacre of her family, she had to escape the murderers in the middle of the worst blizzard in centuries… and she was only 5!

Fast forward twelve years and Bobbi Jo dreams of starting a new life away from the trauma of her past and the antipathy of pitiless relatives.

The nightmare isn't over… but perhaps the tables have turned…

Vindicta - when death isn't retribution enough…

Corrupt Covenant

A pledge of eternal peace and prosperity sounds too good to refuse… unless, of course, the pledge comes from an immortal dragon.

A contract established in exchange for a king's life and the protection of his lineage should have expired when a desperate queen, facing hordes baying for her destruction, loses faith in the oath… but evil has a long memory.

Trapped for a millennium in a sarcophagus at the bottom of the Danube, death lay beyond the queen's grasp until the day nature, fate, and a mysterious archaeologist joined forces to dredge her from her grave.

A life revived. A liegeman doomed to be reborn until he saves his queen. A dragon who has not forgiven an act of betrayal.

Can two souls, separated for a millennium, break the corrupt covenant, or are they fated to dance to the dragon's tune, for eternity?

The Hunters - Dystopian Fiction

Echoes & Illusions - Book 1

Twenty years after a global plague, the remnants of civilisation struggle to eke out an existence in a world where humanity is secondary to survival.

On the outskirts of a once vibrant Rome, Gabriel tends his vineyard. From dawn to dusk, he strives to carve out a living, while caring for Bianca, his heavily pregnant wife.

Life might be tough, but at least he had an income, meagre though it was. Trouble seemed a distant memory, until the day he notices their neighbours are not at work in the adjacent fields.

A gruesome discovery sparks a chain of events to rival the conflicts Rome witnessed at the height of its power. Gabriel and Bianca must pit their wits and their lives against a formidable opponent, in an attempt prevent an atrocity none could have predicted.

A bond, forged in a snowy field and strengthened in a city under siege, is put to the ultimate test.

In a world of echoes and illusions, is their love strong enough to surmount the odds, or will it crumble to dust like the empire their enemies are striving to replicate?

***

Smoke & Mirrors - Book Two

In the aftermath of their fiery clash, an uneasy truce forged between Sophia's Hunters and the Dwellers of Rome allowed life to resume its relatively untroubled rhythm... almost...

… but history warns, it is never a good idea to become complacent.

To the north, a new nightmare materialises. Supported by a band of vindictive acolytes, Carlyle Worthington, the self-proclaimed Pope of Bologna, is determined bring the disparate territories of Italy under his authority and has no hesitation in neutralising anyone who dare thwart his ambition.

As the winds of destruction gain momentum, is the fragile accord strong enough to unite the erstwhile enemies against a common foe, or will the Pope divide and conquer?

Can the fledgling alliance crush the insidious advance, and expose Worthington's fear mongering as little more than smoke and mirrors before evil prevails?

The Sela Helsdatter Saga

A Flip of the Coin - Book One

What happens in Helheim *never* stays in Helheim.

Sela Helsdatter wishes it would. Punished for allowing her quest for power to rule her actions, she has endured eons of torment.

The flip of a coin seems to offer some hope of redemption but, tasked with ridding the world of her erstwhile captor and lover, escape does not mean freedom.

No problem for a warrior queen… right?

Wrong!

Sela is no longer in ninth century Norðvegr, but twenty-first century New York with all its challenges, and where slightest misstep could spell her doom.

Aided by the most unlikely hero, Sela scours the city for her adversary, who delights in taunting her, determined to drag her back to Hell.

Will she prevail, or will A Flip of the Coin catapult her back to the abyss?

***

Conceived Chaos - Book Two

After ridding the world of her tormentor, and finding the love of her life, Sela Helsdatter could be forgiven for thinking she deserves a little peace.

No such luck!

Marriage to the God of Mischief is a walk in the park compared with the terror about to be unleashed from Valhalla. A diabolical edict from Odin himself sees the nine months pregnant, Sela fleeing from the entire Norse pantheon — with no clue why.

A price on her head and a target on her belly, the only person she can trust is her husband, who is keeping her in the dark.

Does her unborn child hold the key to this Conceived Chaos?

***

Odin's Bane - Book Three

Sela Helsdatter cannot catch a break. Relentless in his jealousy and wrath, Odin is determined that neither Sela nor her infant daughter will survive.

Shattered by loss, and with no time to grieve, Sela has to rely on the one person she believes responsible for her current predicament.

A lost friendship revived, the disparate trio seek refuge in a remote corner of Montana, with the uneasy awareness the child may be the key to their salvation.

Vowing Odin will not harm a hair on her daughter's head, Sela has to use every trick at her disposal to thwart the Norse Deity. At the same time another fiendish subversion threatens the future of humanity.

Will Odin be victorious… or is another power stirring which will prove to be his bane?

***

Valhalla's Doom - Book Four

The obsidian stone with its strange steak of neon blue, hanging on a gold chain around Anna Helsdatter's neck — forged from the magma surrounding Jörmungandr's cave — serves as a reminder of the last terrible battle against an insidious evil. The day, Anna came into her full power to defeat the All Father when he sought to destroy not only her family, but also every one of the Nine Realms.

A stone which, unbeknownst to Anna — currently contending with an even greater challenge, that of being college student — hides its own secret.

Putting her past behind her and, despite contending with a family composed of the most powerful deities on Earth or in Valhalla, all Anna wants to do, is to enjoy being a normal nineteen-year-old.

Then again, things involving the Helsdatters, are anything but normal, and Anna is catapulted into another life-or-death struggle. The only problem is, this time the stakes are higher… and one wrong move could spell disaster — especially when saving Earth, might herald Valhalla's Doom.

Just your typical rock and hard place!

***

Arcane Alchemy

Freya's Fate

A Helsdatter Sage Novella

What happens when the goddess of seduction and love finds herself on the losing end of a romance…to a human no less? She packs up, summons her carriage, and sets off to unravel a mystery which has intrigued her for eons.

Where are the deities of this realm? Have they fallen to their doom, never to be revived?

Freya's odyssey takes her to far-flung temples, ancient ruins, and bustling cities, but she is no closer to resolving the riddle, until she arrives in Dublin. In a land where myth and legend are interwoven with everyday life, Freya teeters on the brink of achieving her goal *and* her happily ever after, only to flee to the very couple who triggered her quest.

An unexpected discovery spurs a repeat performance but, this time, Freya no longer cares about the answer. As far as she is concerned, every last god deserves to be consigned to oblivion.

All she wants is to find peace.

Once again, it hovers… tantalisingly close.

Only to be snatched away…

…for Freya's fate is inextricably linked to the one person she is determined to avoid and, to ignore the not-so-subtle summons for help will lead to tragedy.

Some deities have not vanished, some prowl on the periphery preparing to pounce and, as ever when gods interfere in the lives of mortals, chaos ensues.

It will take more than a touch of arcane alchemy to avert the looming catastrophe.

Lesser of Two Evils

If you ask the average American who they intend to vote for in the next election, inevitably, and almost predictably, their reply will be… THE LESSER OF THE TWO EVILS.

Usually, things even out and saner heads prevail… but what happens when the sitting president tries to tip the scales too far in his narcissistic favor simply to get re-elected?

As the world teeters on the brink of a grim fate, it is up to a lone reporter to prevent that from happening…and to stay alive.

Deadly Incision

From the learned halls of the London Hospital to the squalid, bustling streets of Whitechapel surrounding it, life and death walk hand in glove with one another.

This, somewhat fatalistic, status quo was shattered in the autumn of 1888, when Jack the Ripper prowled the darkness, perfecting his 'skills' on unsuspecting women of the night.

Follow us down these same dark and deadly alleyways to hidden corners and stairwells, stained with blood by the legendary Leather Apron's blade to discover a new twist to his story.

www.ingramcontent.com/pod-product-compliance
Lightning Source LLC
Chambersburg PA
CBHW070357200726

48294CB00003B/957